TRISHA ALEXANDER

FALLING FOR AN OLDER MAN

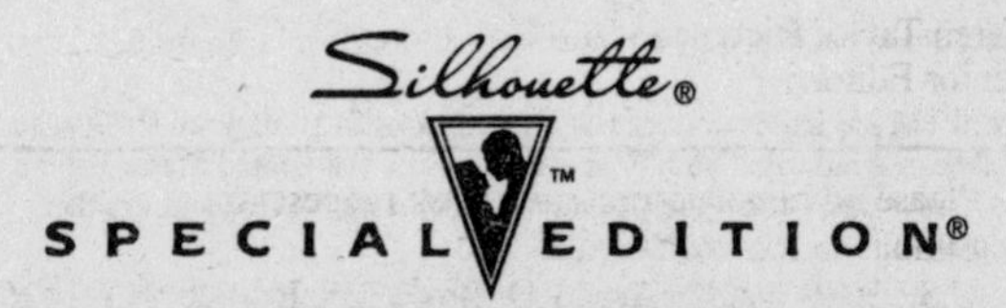

Published by Silhouette Books
America's Publisher of Contemporary Romance

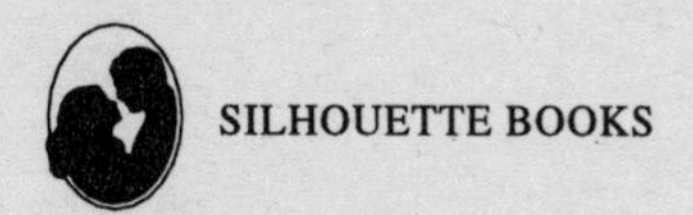

ISBN 0-373-24308-1

FALLING FOR AN OLDER MAN

This edition published by arrangement with Harlequin Books S.A.

Visit us at www.romance.net

Printed in U.S.A.

Books by Trisha Alexander

Silhouette Special Edition

Cinderella Girl #640
When Somebody Loves You #748
When Somebody Needs You #784
Mother of the Groom #801
When Somebody Wants You #822
Here Comes the Groom #845
Say You Love Me #875
What Will the Children Think? #906
Let's Make It Legal #924
The Real Elizabeth Hollister... #940
The Girl Next Door #965
This Child Is Mine #989
**A Bride for Luke* #1024
**A Bride for John* #1047
**A Baby for Rebecca* #1070
Stop the Wedding! #1097
Substitute Bride #1115
With This Wedding Ring #1169
A Mother for Jeffrey #1211
†*Wedding Bells and Mistletoe* #1289
†*Falling for an Older Man* #1308

*Three Brides and a Baby
†Callahans & Kin

TRISHA ALEXANDER

has had a lifelong love affair with books and has always wanted to be a writer. She also loves cats, movies, the ocean, music, Broadway shows, cooking, traveling, being with her family and friends, Cajun food, "Calvin and Hobbes," and getting mail. Trisha and her husband have three grown children, three adorable grandchildren and live in Houston, Texas. Trisha loves to hear from readers. You can write to her at P.O. Box 441603, Houston, TX 77244-1603.

IT'S OUR 20th ANNIVERSARY!

We'll be celebrating all year, continuing with these fabulous titles, on sale in February 2000.

Special Edition

#1303 Man...Mercenary... Monarch
Joan Elliott Pickart

#1304 Dr. Mom and the Millionaire
Christine Flynn

#1305 Who's That Baby?
Diana Whitney

#1306 Cattleman's Courtship
Lois Faye Dyer

#1307 The Marriage Basket
Sharon De Vita

#1308 Falling for an Older Man
Trisha Alexander

Intimate Moments

#985 The Wildes of Wyoming–Chance
Ruth Langan

#986 Wild Ways
Naomi Horton

#987 Mistaken Identity
Merline Lovelace

#988 Family on the Run
Margaret Watson

#989 On Dangerous Ground
Maggie Price

#990 Catch Me If You Can
Nina Bruhns

Romance

#1426 Waiting for the Wedding
Carla Cassidy

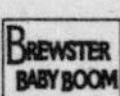

#1427 Bringing Up Babies
Susan Meier

#1428 The Family Diamond
Moyra Tarling

#1429 Simon Says...Marry Me!
Myrna Mackenzie

#1430 The Double Heart Ranch
Leanna Wilson

#1431 If the Ring Fits...
Melissa McClone

Desire

#1273 A Bride for Jackson Powers
Dixie Browning

#1274 Sheikh's Temptation
Alexandra Sellers

#1275 The Daddy Salute
Maureen Child

#1276 Husband for Keeps
Kate Little

#1277 The Magnificent M.D.
Carol Grace

#1278 Jesse Hawk: Brave Father
Sheri WhiteFeather

Chapter One

"Sheila, love, could you come in here, please?"

"Be right there, Dad." Sheila Callahan finished inputting the last few figures to the spreadsheet on her computer screen, saved the work, then headed into her father's office.

Patrick Callahan, Sr., her father and the president of Callahan Construction Company, sat behind a scarred oak desk, scribbling something on a legal pad.

He looked up when she entered and smiled. "Now that we have that school job, we need to hire a few more men. I want you to put an ad in the *Rainbow's End Register* and in the Austin *American Statesman.*"

"All right. How much and what kind of experience are you looking for?"

Her father grimaced and leaned back in his swivel chair, which squeaked in protest. Sheila smiled. Every piece of furniture in the office had seen better days, for Patrick didn't believe in spending money on what he called window dressing.

''With the building boom going on in Austin, I don't think we're going to get men with experience, not unless we're willing to pay a lot more than they can make elsewhere, and we can't afford that. Say we'll train.''

''We'll train?'' Sheila echoed in disbelief. She couldn't remember a time when they had ever hired inexperienced workers. In fact, the only people who had ever learned on the job were her brothers.

Patrick sighed. ''I know, but I don't see as how we have a choice anymore.''

Sheila nodded. She started to return to her office, then stopped in midstride. Turning, she saw that her father had already shifted his attention back to the legal pad and whatever it was that he'd been working on when she'd entered. ''Dad...''

''Hmm?'' He didn't look up.

''Since you're now willing to train workers,'' she said softly, ''why not give *me* a chance?''

He sighed heavily and lifted his blue gaze to hers. ''Sheila, don't start that again.''

''Come on, Dad, all I'm asking for is a chance. Let me show you that I can do the work.''

Her father shook his head, his mouth settling into the stubborn line she knew so well. The line that

said *I've made up my mind and nothing you do or say will make me change it.*

"You're not being fair," she said in the calmest, most reasonable tone she could muster. "Why should the boys be taken into the business and not me?"

"What are you talking about? You *have* been taken into the business."

"Sure, as the office manager." Which, in her opinion, was just a glorified bookkeeping job. There was nothing wrong with bookkeeping, if that was the kind of work a person liked to do, but it bored Sheila. "I want to do more. I want to actually get out there and build things. I want to be a crew chief or a foreman like Keith and Kevin, Patrick, Rory and Glenn," she added, naming all her brothers. "I want to have a say in how things are done and how the business is run." When her father didn't answer, she rushed on. "Why should I be treated differently just because I'm a woman? Don't you know that women are succeeding in all kinds of professions where it used to be thought only men could do the job? They're cops and firefighters and factory workers. They drill for oil. They serve in the Army and Navy and—"

"Enough, Sheila!" her father thundered. "How many times do we have to cover the same ground? The answer is no. Now I'm busy, and I don't want to hear another word on the subject." So saying, he got up, turned his back to her, opened the top drawer of his filing cabinet and began searching for a file.

Sheila counted to ten. She was so blasted sick of being treated like a child. Glaring at her father's back, she thought of a dozen things she might counter with. But after fuming a few more minutes, she swallowed every one of them. It never did any good to argue with him. He would just dig in his heels all the harder.

Remember, it's easier to catch flies with honey than it is with vinegar.

Her mother's advice was sound, Sheila knew, but she was so frustrated. Her father was so implacable, and so old-fashioned. How long was she supposed to wait for him to join the twenty-first century?

Sheila walked back to her office and plopped dejectedly into her own ancient swivel chair. She stared at the spreadsheet on the screen. She had worked as the office manager for the family's construction company ever since graduating from business school four years ago. Despite her disparaging tone to her father, she knew hers was a good job. It just wasn't the job for her. She wasn't cut out to work in an office. She never had been, and this experience had shown her that she never would be. But try explaining *that* to her father.

Sheila was an outdoor girl. Physical activity had always been her choice over indoor pursuits. Even as a kid, she'd preferred playing football with her older brothers than with the dolls her family had insisted on buying her. Those poor dolls, she thought with a wry smile. They'd gathered inch-thick dust waiting for her to take an interest in them.

From the time she'd been old enough to understand what the family business was all about, she'd wanted to work on one of the construction crews, the same way her brothers did. But her father wouldn't hear of it, and he'd been backed up by her brothers.

"A construction crew is no place for a woman," her father had said every time she broached the subject. "The language, the atmosphere, the danger of the work...women don't belong there."

"Dad's right," her brothers echoed. Not a one of them had been on her side, not even Glenn, the brother she was closest to, both in age and in every other way. It was funny about her and Glenn. They were completely opposite in temperament. Sheila was impulsive, restless, quick-tempered. Glenn, on the other hand, was thoughtful, patient, and the most easygoing guy you'd ever want to meet. Maybe that was exactly why they got along so well, she thought now, because they *were* so different. But despite their closeness, Glenn had not stuck up for her when it came to her wish to work construction the way he did.

So Sheila had bowed to pressure and gone to business college. But she'd never been able to conquer her frustration or her longing for a different life. Most days that longing and frustration were buried. Today they had risen to the surface and refused to be pushed down again.

Just then, she heard the outside door open. She turned to greet the newcomer, and her heart gave its

customary leap at the sight of Jack Kinsella, her brother Kevin's best friend and the other main source of frustration in Sheila's life. Unfortunately for Sheila, she had been in love with Jack for more years than she cared to count, but Jack never saw her as anything but Kevin's kid sister.

"Hey, squirt," he said now, giving her his killer smile accompanied by a wink.

"Hello, Jack." Although the despised nickname only added to her simmering anger, if Sheila said anything, Jack would just use the sobriquet more frequently. "What can I do for you?" she added coolly. Pride had dictated a long time ago that she would never give Jack any clue to the way she felt about him.

"Just wondered if you had the payroll ready yet," he said in his lazy drawl, the one that made her nether regions turn to Silly Putty. His hazel eyes always seemed to carry a glint of some hidden amusement.

She raised her eyebrows. "I can't believe it. You're broke *again?*"

He shrugged, not in the least offended by her crack. "Hey, what can I say?"

"Nothing," she muttered under her breath. She knew full well why he was always broke. She wondered whether the woman in question was another blonde. They usually were. Tall, leggy, busty blondes. Sheila wasn't tall or leggy or busty. "The checks won't be ready until four." Turning away from the sight of him, she resumed making entries

into the spreadsheet. She knew he'd left the office by the sound of the door closing, and it was only then that she gave way to the unhappiness seeing him had caused.

Maybe she needed to go away. To quit this job she disliked so much and leave Rainbow's End.

I could get a job in Austin or Houston or even San Antonio. I'd still be close to home, but at least I wouldn't have to go through the torture of seeing Jack constantly.

The idea gathered force as the afternoon wore on. Why not? If she *had* to work at an office job, why not work someplace where she could take carpentry or bricklaying or electrical courses at night? In Sheila's opinion, the lack of educational opportunities was the biggest drawback to living in a small town like Rainbow's End. They weren't completely deprived, of course. They did have a community college. In fact, her sister-in-law Susan had worked there for a couple of years. But there were no trade schools nearby.

If Sheila moved away, she could enroll in one of those schools, learn a useful skill, and then she could probably get a job in construction with some other company. That'd show her family, she thought with rising enthusiasm. That'd show them once and for all.

Man, that Sheila sure had turned into a babe. Jack watched his crew finish placing the final planks across the floor joists on the third of the dozen or

so houses they were building in the newest and hottest area in town. She'd been on his mind ever since he'd returned to the construction site after lunch.

When was it, he wondered, that he'd begun to think of her as a sexy woman instead of Kevin's little sister? He couldn't remember exactly when the change in his thinking had occurred and guessed it didn't matter, anyway, because thinking about her was as far as he'd ever get.

Sheila was off-limits, big-time. He didn't care how gorgeous her dark hair or her creamy complexion or her wide gray eyes were. He didn't care how much her curvy body and her perfect legs turned him on. Sure, he'd love to get his hands on her. What guy wouldn't? But getting anywhere near Sheila would be asking for a heap of trouble.

Jack knew himself too well. He didn't want to be tied down. Marriage was for suckers. As far as he was concerned, marriage went against all the laws of nature. Man was never meant to be hitched permanently to one woman, even a woman as delectable as Sheila Callahan.

Hell, all a guy had to do was look around him. Most marriages were a disaster. His own parents were a prime example. As far back as Jack could remember, his mother and father had hated each other. They'd stuck together until Jack's younger brother, Mike, was out of high school, then they'd finally split. Now they were both happier than Jack had ever seen them.

And then there was Mike himself. He'd gotten

caught early, because he'd been stupid. He'd knocked up a girl, ended up marrying her because her parents practically put a gun to his head, and the marriage hadn't lasted four years. Now Mike, who was only thirty-one, was saddled with child support for two kids he hardly ever saw because his ex-wife had moved to Denver. Not that Mike had ever complained. He loved his kids, but it sure wasn't a good situation.

Jack could have named dozens of examples of bad marriages, whereas he could only think of a handful that seemed to work, namely Old Man Callahan's and those of the two of his sons that were married—Patrick and Keith. Of course, Jack thought wryly, the jury was still out on Keith's marriage, because he and Susan hadn't been together long enough for a real test.

Yep. Sheila Callahan was definitely hands-off. She was not the kind of girl you fooled around with, then dropped. She was a diamond-ring, picket-fences kind of girl. And even if she hadn't been, she was the sister of his best friend. A friend Jack wanted to keep. A friend who would *kill* him if he messed with Sheila with anything other than honorable intentions.

Too bad, he thought with regret as the shift ended and he headed for the trailer that housed their on-site office. Some sites didn't have offices, but because the company expected to be building houses here at Willowbend for the foreseeable future, Old Man Callahan had decided it made sense to have a

place where Jack could do paperwork, deal with any personnel problems and make phone calls in privacy. Emblazoned on the side of the trailer was the company motto: CALLAHAN CONSTRUCTION: WE DO IT ALL.

Jack had heard the story at least a dozen times. How the first Callahan had started the company. How he had started out building cupboards or adding rooms to existing houses or doing repair work. And how the company had eventually evolved into the full-service construction company it now was. They no longer did minor repairs but the motto had remained unchanged. Because so many people had discovered Rainbow's End, the majority of their work now was building houses, but they had built all kinds of other structures: offices, apartments, restaurants, clinics, the community college, and recently they'd won a bid to build the new high school in Pollero, a nearby town. It was a thriving company, one Jack was proud to be a part of.

Entering the trailer, Jack made a few calls, then locked up, climbed into his pickup truck and headed back to the main office to get his paycheck. Luckily, he thought as his mind veered back to Sheila, he didn't have to see much of her, so he could keep his testosterone levels under control. Yet he couldn't help feeling disappointed when he walked into the office and saw her desk cleaned off and her computer shut down. She'd gone home early, because it wasn't five o'clock yet. Maybe she had a hot date. He frowned, vaguely bothered by the idea of her

seeing some guy who was bound to want to get into her pants. What red-blooded American male *wouldn't* want to get into her pants?

"Hey, Jack, you gonna move out of the way or what?"

Jack whipped around and met Kevin Callahan's amused blue eyes. Sheepishly, Jack realized he'd been blocking access to the mail cubicles Sheila used for their messages, paychecks and company-generated information. "Sorry." He reached for his pay envelope, then moved aside so Kevin could get his.

"We goin' to Pot O' Gold tonight?" Kevin said. The local pub was their usual Friday night haunt.

Jack shrugged. "Sure."

The two walked outside together. It was late October, and the weather had finally turned cool after one of the hottest summers on record. Jack liked this time of year best—before the really cold weather set in.

"So what time do you want to go?" Kevin asked.

"Around eight?"

"Want me to pick you up?"

"Why don't we just meet there?"

Kevin grinned. "Good thinking. One of us might get lucky tonight."

Because it was expected of him, Jack grinned, too. Yet he couldn't dispel the vague feeling of discontent brought on by his earlier thoughts of Sheila. As he drove home, he told himself to quit thinking about her, yet he couldn't shake his mind free of

her. He wondered if she *was* dating anyone. He couldn't imagine a knockout like her *not* seeing someone.

By now, he'd reached the small apartment complex he'd called home for the past seventeen years. He knew all his friends thought he squandered his money and couldn't afford to buy a house or live anywhere better, and since he believed his finances were his own business, he never corrected them.

Truth was, he could have afforded to buy any house in Rainbow's End. For cash. Because contrary to popular belief, Jack did not spend every penny he earned. In fact, starting with his first paycheck at sixteen, he had faithfully saved a percentage of his salary. That was one good habit he'd learned from his father, who'd always said a man should pay himself first. Jack had begun with a bank savings account but quickly realized he wasn't going to earn much interest that way, so for a long time he'd been investing in stocks and mutual funds. Even Kevin, who knew him better than anyone, would have been amazed to know what Jack's financial portfolio looked like.

Jack's aim was to retire at fifty. He only had thirteen more years to go. Then he planned to head for the Caribbean, maybe buy himself a houseboat, and spend the rest of his life fishing and enjoying life. Who knew? At the rate his investments were growing, he might be able to accomplish his goal even earlier, say when he turned forty-five.

Reminded of his objectives, he finally pushed

thoughts of Sheila out of his mind, because nowhere in this plan was there room for a woman like her.

"C'mon, Sheila. Why don't you want to go to Pot O' Gold tonight?"

Sheila was talking on the phone to her best friend, Carrie Ferguson. She wished she could be honest—say that she didn't relish the idea of spending the evening watching Jack ogle other women—but not even Carrie knew how Sheila felt about Jack, and Sheila didn't intend to tell her. Nope. No pity parties for her. "I don't know, I just don't," she hedged.

"But what else is there to do in this one-horse town?"

Carrie's complaint was one Sheila had heard more times than she could count. "If you feel that way, I don't know why you don't move to Austin."

"It costs too much to live there, that's why."

Sheila knew money wasn't the real reason. The real reason Carrie didn't move away was she was scared to leave Rainbow's End. She'd never admit it, but Sheila knew it was true. Rainbow's End was the known. Austin was the unknown. Sheila wished Carrie would just admit it, then maybe they could talk about her fears. "What if I told you I was thinking of moving to Austin myself?"

"Sheila!" Carrie squealed. "Really?"

"Really."

"Gee, what brought that on?"

"Oh, you know. Same old, same old."

"Did you have an argument with your father again?"

"Yeah," Sheila said glumly.

"Well, shoot, if you move to Austin, I'll move, too. We can share an apartment! Oh, Sheila! It'll be such fun to live together, don't you think?"

Sheila wasn't so sure about that. Carrie wasn't the neatest person in the world, plus, much as Sheila liked her, she was the kind of person who needed constant diversion. Sheila knew for a fact that Carrie hadn't cracked a single book since high school. Sheila was a people person, too, but she could also entertain herself quite contentedly as long as she had a good book to read.

"And Austin's close enough that we can come home whenever we want," Carrie rushed on, oblivious to Sheila's lack of response. "Oh, it'll be perfect! Just perfect! When're you going to tell your folks?"

"It's not a done deal yet."

"What do you mean?"

"I mean, I said I was *thinking* of moving to Austin, not that I had decided."

"Oh."

Sheila couldn't help smiling at the sudden deflation of Carrie's enthusiasm. "I want to talk to my father about it first."

"What are you going to say?"

"I'm going to give him one last chance. Tell him if he'll let me start learning the business, hands on,

then I'll stay. But if he won't change his mind, then I'm going somewhere else."

"Do you think there's a chance he'll relent?"

Sheila sighed. "Honestly? I don't know. He's so stubborn."

"When are you going to talk to him?"

"This weekend, I think. I'll go over to the house early on Sunday." Sundays were a command performance at her parents' home, a time when the entire family gathered for dinner and family time together. It was funny, Sheila thought, but she'd never resented the weekly obligation, the way so many of her contemporaries did when their families expected them to take part in family activities. Sheila might chafe at the way her father sometimes treated her, but she still loved him and her mother. And although her brothers had made a life's work out of teasing her, she loved them, too.

And she was crazy about her nieces, especially the newest one, little Megan, the six-month-old daughter of Sheila's brother Keith and his wife, Susan. Yeah, she had a pretty nice family. She would miss them if she moved away, because visiting once or twice a month just wouldn't be the same as the daily contact she had now.

"So if we're not going to Pot O' Gold, what are we going to do tonight?" Carrie said, bringing the conversation back to its original starting point.

"Why don't you come over? We can rent some movies, and pop some popcorn or send out for a pizza. Just have a girls' night."

"I've been in all week. I want to go out and have some fun."

"I'm sorry, Carrie. I'm just not in the mood. Tell you what. You go on to Pot O' Gold, and I'll just stay home and go to bed early. I'm tired, anyway." She should go work out at the gym—she hadn't been since Tuesday—but she could do that tomorrow morning.

"You don't mind?"

"Nope. Not at all."

"Well, okay. Maybe I'll give Lisa a call, see if she wants to go. That is, if you're sure..."

"I'm sure."

For the rest of the evening, and periodically throughout the day on Saturday, Sheila thought about their conversation regarding a possible move to Austin. The more she thought about it, the more she hoped her father would finally see the light, because she really didn't want to move away from her family and friends. Yes, Austin was close and she could come home every weekend, if she wanted, but then she'd have to stay with her parents, because she certainly couldn't afford to keep her apartment in Rainbow's End if she had to pay for a place in Austin.

That would never work. She guessed she could stay with Jan and Patrick when she visited. At forty, Patrick was her oldest brother, but Sheila had always felt close to him and his wife. She knew they wouldn't mind having her any time she wanted to be with them, but even with a four-bedroom home,

they were crowded, since they had four daughters, two of whom were teenagers.

By Sunday morning, she was on pins and needles to get the talk behind her. Leaving her apartment at eight, she headed for Holy Family. Sheila sang in the church choir, and even though the service didn't begin until nine-thirty, they practiced for an hour before putting on their robes and going over to the church.

Singing in the choir at Holy Family was something else she'd really miss if she moved. She'd been with the choir for two years now. Rehearsals and singing on Sundays and special days were an important part of her week. She sighed as she pulled into the church parking lot. Why did life have to be so difficult?

Sheila's parents always attended the nine-thirty Mass, and today was no exception. She spotted them sitting in their usual seats in the second row of the center section. Her mother smiled when their eyes met, and Sheila smiled back. She tried to catch her father's eye, too, but he wasn't looking in her direction. Soon after, the opening notes of the entrance hymn resonated from the organ, and everyone stood to sing.

When Mass was over, Sheila gathered up her music and headed in the direction of her parents, who were talking to their neighbors. Normally, Sheila would have gone directly to the rehearsal hall to change out of her robe, but she wanted to be sure her parents were going straight home today.

As she approached the group, she did a double take, for moving toward them from the opposite direction was none other than Jack Kinsella.

Jack? At Mass? Would wonders never cease?

Rose Callahan, who was facing his way, said, "Jack! How good to see you. Come here and give me a hug."

Grinning, Jack complied. His amused eyes met Sheila's over her mother's shoulder. "Hey, squirt."

"Hello, Jack." Sheila inwardly berated her wayward heart, even as she gave him an unruffled smile. Why *couldn't* she keep her emotions under control when Jack was anywhere near?

Her mother—who Sheila thought looked lovely in a cranberry-red wool dress—released Jack and turned to smile at Sheila. "Honey, the music was beautiful this morning."

"Yes, it was," Sheila's father agreed, giving her a shoulder hug and smiling down at her proudly. He was always proud of her when she did proper, ladylike things, she thought wryly.

The neighbors, Mr. and Mrs. Caselli, echoed her parents' sentiments.

"Thanks." Sheila smiled at the Casellis. After a few moments of chitchat, they said they had to be going; they were meeting their daughter and her husband for brunch. When they were gone, Sheila looked at her mother and said, "I was wondering...um, are you and Dad going straight home?"

"Yes, we are," her mother answered. "Why?"

"I thought I'd come over early."

''Good. That'll give us a chance to talk before everyone else gets there and the place turns into a madhouse.''

Sheila smiled. Her mother loved what she called a madhouse. Nothing else made Rose as happy as being surrounded by her family.

Rose turned to Jack. ''Jack, why don't you come for dinner today? You haven't been in a long time.''

Sheila's jaw tightened. That was all she needed, especially today, when she was already on tenterhooks. Say no, she commanded Jack silently.

''And I've been missing your wonderful cooking, too,'' Jack said. ''Especially your rolls.'' Rose's melt-in-your-mouth yeast rolls were a mainstay at family dinners.

Rose smiled happily. She loved to be complimented on her rolls. ''I'll make extra if you come.''

''Who can resist that kind of offer?'' Jack said. Briefly, his eyes met Sheila's.

Although she was inwardly cringing, Sheila gave him another who-cares? smile, then said her goodbyes and left. Twenty-five minutes later, she pulled into the driveway of her parents' two-story home.

Well, here goes, she thought, trying to rid herself of her butterflies. She hoped her father would be reasonable. Surely he wouldn't want her to move away. He never wanted any of them to move away. Sheila remembered how upset he'd been when Keith had moved to Alaska and how he had continually tried to talk Keith into coming back. And when

Keith finally *had* come back, her father had been over the moon.

No, he wouldn't want Sheila to move away. But he also wouldn't want her to be on a construction crew, either. He would try to talk Sheila out of both options.

Well, she wasn't going to be talked out of her decision. No matter what her father said, she would not back down. He would have to choose.

Taking a deep breath, she walked into her parents' house.

Chapter Two

Sheila found her mother in the kitchen. The windows were steamed up from all the cooking, and the tempting aroma of roasting meat filled the air. Rose, a checkered apron protecting her dress, stood peeling potatoes at the counter. She looked up and smiled.

"What's in the oven?" Sheila asked.

"Pork tenderloin."

"It smells wonderful." Sheila opened the refrigerator and helped herself to a diet drink. "Where's Dad?" She popped the top and took a swallow.

Rose inclined her head toward the backyard. "Out back with Fritz." Fritz was their ten-year-old Irish setter.

"Think I'll go out and see him."

Her mother's blue eyes were thoughtful as they studied Sheila. "Is something wrong, honey?"

Sheila shook her head. "No. I just need to talk to Dad. It's about work."

"Oh." But Rose didn't look convinced.

She knew her mother was watching her as she headed toward the back door.

Sheila found her father sitting on the back stoop. From the pile of red hair that lay on a newspaper by his feet, she figured he'd been grooming the dog. Fritz, who was nosing at the base of the fence separating her parents' yard from their back neighbors', came bounding over to greet her.

Sheila sat down next to her father and let Fritz lap the back of her hand for a minute before saying, "Okay, that's enough." She patted the dog's head, and after a moment, he loped off toward the fence again. "Dad, I came over early because I wanted to talk to you."

Patrick's eyes reflected concern. "What's wrong, love? Got a problem?"

She was amazed at how quickly he'd forgotten their argument, but she guessed she shouldn't be surprised. What they'd talked about on Friday was only important to her. "Yes, you could say that."

He put his arm around her. "Tell your old dad all about it."

"Well, for starters, I'm very unhappy," she said quietly.

"Ah, Sheila. I'm sorry. What's wrong?"

"Come on, Daddy, you *know* what's wrong. I've

tried to talk to you about this subject over and over again, but you always get mad and say you don't want to talk about it anymore.''

Stiffening, he withdrew his arm. ''Sheila, not again. Didn't we just have this conversation Friday?''

She placed her hand on his forearm in a placating gesture. ''Yes, Daddy, we did. And I've been thinking about it ever since. Will you please just listen to what I have to say?''

He sighed.

''Just hear me out, okay? That's not so much to ask, is it?''

Another sigh. ''All right, Sheila. All right. Say your piece.'' His tone was that of long-suffering patience.

''Well, as I said, I've been doing a lot of thinking. You've made it very clear you don't want me to work on one of our construction crews. I know exactly how you feel. That you think it's no place for a woman. But I'm not happy working in the office. It's not the kind of work I want to spend the rest of my life doing.''

''I don't want you to spend the rest of your life working in any office, either. I want you to get married. Have babies.''

Sheila had decided earlier today that no matter what her father said, she would not lose her temper. So her voice was calm when she answered. ''I'd like to get married someday and have babies, too, but that has nothing to do with what I'm talking about.''

''I think it has *everything* to do—''

''Please let me finish.'' When he subsided into silence, she continued. ''Anyway, I've made a decision.'' She waited a heartbeat. ''I have decided that since you won't let me learn the building part of the business and work on one of your crews, I'm going to cash in my savings, move to Austin and enroll in a trade school. Then, when I graduate, I'll have the skills to go to work for another construction company there or somewhere else.''

''You're *what?*'' her father exploded, drawing back and giving her a look of incredulity. ''That's the craziest thing I've ever heard.''

Don't lose your temper. ''You may think it's crazy, but it's my life, and that's what I intend to do.''

He stared at her, his blue eyes still as bright, intense and intimidating as they had been when she was a small child. ''You'd leave your family?''

''It's not what I want to do, but it looks to me as if I have no choice.'' She steeled herself not to look away, even though she'd never known anyone to win a staring contest with her dad.

His jaw clenched. ''Sheila, blackmailing me isn't going to work.''

''I'm sorry you see it as blackmailing you, Daddy. That's not what I intended. I just thought, if you knew what I plan to do, you might have a change of heart. It only seemed fair to tell you first,'' she added with dignity.

''Call it what you like. I'm not going to have a

change of heart. Even if a construction crew was a suitable place for a woman, you couldn't do the work.''

''I *can* do the work. I can do anything my brothers can do. Have you ever watched us play football? Do you know how much I work out? I can do more sit-ups than Glenn. I can do more push-ups than Kevin. I'm strong!''

''Football, sit-ups, push-ups,'' he scoffed. ''That's nothing. That's child's play compared to working construction. Believe me, Sheila, all you'd have to do is spend one day digging trenches—which is the way all your brothers started out—and you'd change your tune.''

''Try me.''

He shook his head.

There was that stubborn set chin again. Oh, he made her so mad! Gritting her teeth, she answered in even tones. ''And that's it? That's your final word on the subject?''

''That's my final word.''

''Fine,'' she said, rising and dusting off her black slacks. ''In that case you will have my typed letter of resignation on your desk tomorrow. I'll give you two weeks notice, the same as any other employee.'' So saying, she swung on her heel and marched back into the house.

Pretending not to see her mother's startled expression, Sheila strode past her and down the hall into the guest bathroom. She didn't allow her emotions to spill over until the door was securely locked.

With trembling hands, she brushed away angry tears. Her heart was beating too fast, and looking in the mirror, she could see that her face was flushed.

She couldn't believe how bullheaded her father was. Why wouldn't he at least give her a chance? If he was so all-fired sure she couldn't do the job, why didn't he prove he was right and she was wrong?

It hurt to know he would rather see her leave Rainbow's End than give an inch. It hurt a lot.

But if that was the way he wanted it, then that was the way it would be.

Jack was looking forward to dinner with the Callahans. Not only did Rose Callahan put on a great feed, but he enjoyed seeing the whole family together in a relaxed atmosphere.

He chuckled. Maybe *relaxed atmosphere* and *Callahans* was an oxymoron. Come to think of it, he had never known the clan to gather without an eruption of fireworks of some kind.

He'd been invited for one o'clock, so at ten till, he parked his truck in front of the attractive, two-story house and walked to the front door. Almost everyone was already there, he saw by the lineup of cars and trucks in the drive and on the street.

Patrick, Jr. opened the door and smiled. "Hey, Jack. C'mon in."

The men of the family were in the den, where a big-screen TV—a gift from the brothers to their father two Christmases ago—was showing a Dallas

Cowboys football game. Jack saw that of the brothers, only Keith was missing. He greeted everyone and asked about Keith.

"They're coming," Kevin said. "Keith called and said they were running late. Something about the baby teething and keeping them up half the night."

Jack grimaced. "See why I don't want to get married?"

Kevin answered with a grin. Kevin and Jack had been best friends since elementary school, and they had the same mind-set when it came to marriage. In fact, if possible, Kevin was even more of a confirmed bachelor than Jack, because his feelings about marriage had nothing to do with the statistics and failure rate. He always said he simply didn't want to be tied down to anyone. He liked doing what he wanted to do without having to answer to someone else.

"The day I let some female tell me how to spend my money is the day when hell freezes over," he'd said at least a hundred times.

Jack wondered about the other brothers. Rory was thirty-one and Glenn was twenty-eight, and neither one was involved in a serious relationship, either, much to their mother's chagrin.

And then, of course, there was Sheila. Remembering Sheila, Jack said, "Guess I'll go out to the kitchen and say hello to the women."

"Get yourself a beer while you're there," Kevin said offhandedly.

"Kevin," Patrick, Sr. admonished. "That's no way to treat a guest."

"Hell, Jack's not a guest. He's family," Kevin answered, lounging back into his chair.

Jack smiled and walked to the kitchen. Voices and laughter, accompanied by delicious smells, would have guided him even if he hadn't known the way.

"Hello," he said upon entering the room.

Seven pairs of female eyes turned his way. Rose and Jan, Patrick, Jr.'s wife, were standing side by side at the stove. Sheila had just opened the refrigerator. And Jan's four daughters were in various stages of food preparation at the big round kitchen table. All except Sheila gave him a big smile and happy hello. Sheila smiled, but he could tell the smile was forced. He immediately knew something was bothering her and wondered what it was.

"Gram says men aren't allowed in the kitchen," piped up Allene, Jan and Patrick's eight-year-old charmer.

Her older sister Jana, sixteen, grinned at him. "Yeah. She says you're just in the way."

Briana, the twelve-year-old, giggled. And Katie, who was turning into a real looker at fourteen, gave him a shy smile.

"Now, now, girls," Rose said, laughing.

"All I'm gonna do is get myself a beer, then I'm outta here," Jack said. But he laughed, too.

Sheila reached into the refrigerator and handed him a can.

"Thanks." She looked great today, if subdued, in

trim black slacks and a soft, silky gray blouse the exact color of her eyes.

"Sure," she said. Her eyes had none of their usual luster.

Yes, something was definitely bothering her, Jack thought as he walked back to the den to join the guys. He only half paid attention to the game and the occasional comments of men because he kept wondering about her. Later, as they all sat around the dining room table, he studied Sheila surreptitiously. She was very quiet, which wasn't like her at all. She spoke when spoken to, but didn't offer anything, even when the conversation turned to the coming election and the fact that a woman from Rainbow's End was running for sheriff.

"I don't care what anybody says," Patrick, Sr. pronounced. "Women don't belong in law enforcement." His laserlike blue gaze settled on Sheila. "Just like they don't belong on construction crews."

"Patrick," Rose said softly, giving him a quelling look, which he pointedly ignored.

"Well, they don't," he repeated firmly.

Two bright spots of color tinged Sheila's cheeks, but instead of the fiery retort she usually made when confronted with her father's implacable stance regarding the suitability of women in what he considered men's roles, she just set her lips in a grim line and continued to eat.

Very interesting, Jack thought. Very, very interesting. Looking across the table, his eye caught

Kevin's. An unspoken question passed between them.

Kevin shrugged, as if to say, *Don't ask me. I don't have a clue.*

Eventually, the talk turned to something else, but Jack continued to study Sheila whenever he could do so without calling attention to his scrutiny. And he noticed that her mother's troubled glance kept settling on Sheila, too. But if the others noticed, they weren't letting on, for her lack of participation in the conversation didn't temper their normal lively interchange.

By dessert, though—a rich chocolate pecan cake that Jack ate two servings of—Sheila seemed more relaxed, for she turned to Susan, Keith's wife of two years, and said, "Susan, Megan is getting cuter every day."

Susan brightened with pleasure. "She is, isn't she?"

She and Keith exchanged sappy looks, amusing Jack, although even he had to admit their baby was a cutie, with fat cheeks, a happy smile and bright blue eyes exactly like her daddy's.

Susan's son by her first marriage, Scott, who was twelve, reached back and picked up his sister's teething ring, which had fallen off her high chair tray. Funny, Jack thought, watching the boy, but he had those same intensely blue Callahan eyes. If a person didn't know his parentage, they'd be hard put to believe Keith *wasn't* his father. It was plain to see, too, that Keith was crazy about the kid. Yeah,

maybe this marriage *would* work out. It did seem to have a lot going for it.

"Remember, I said I'd baby-sit anytime you want," Sheila told Susan. Then, suddenly, her smile faded, as if she'd just thought of something, and the thought wasn't pleasant. But as Jack watched, she visibly forced herself to smile again. What the devil was going on with her? In all the years he'd known her, he'd never seen her act this way.

Glenn, who was sitting next to Sheila, leaned over and said something in a low tone. She shook her head, and just for an instant, her eyes met Jack's. The bleak look he saw jolted him. Up until that moment, he had thought Sheila was angry or upset about something. But now he realized she was sad. Sad and hurting. Something stirred inside, and he had the strongest urge to comfort her.

Don't be an idiot, he told himself. She's fine. Quit thinking about comforting her. In fact, quit thinking about her, period.

Remember, she's off-limits.

Sheila couldn't wait for the meal to be over. She'd decided earlier that she was going to leave for home as soon as the table was cleared.

So once the dishes had all been carried off to the kitchen, she helped load the dishwasher and put the leftover food away, then turned to her mother and said, "Sorry to run out early, Mom, but I'm not feeling good, so I think I'm going to go home."

"Oh, honey, I'm sorry," her mother said. "I hope you're not coming down with a cold."

Jan and Susan echoed her mother's sentiments.

"Nah," Sheila said, "it's just cramps."

"I wondered why you were so quiet during dinner," Jan said, giving her a commiserating smile.

"I hate cramps," Susan said. "That was the best thing about being pregnant. Well, the *next* best thing. The best thing was getting Megan as a result." She gave the baby—who was happily ensconced in the playpen Sheila's mother kept in the corner of the kitchen—a loving smile.

For some reason, Susan's happiness was tough to watch today. Maybe because Sheila wasn't sure she'd ever find that kind of contentment.

"You go on home, honey," Rose said, "we'll finish up here."

After poking her head into the dining room, where the men still sat around the table exchanging war stories, and saying a quick goodbye, Sheila made her escape. She was certain her father knew exactly why she was leaving, but she didn't care. All she wanted was to go home and stoke her entirely justified anger and try to forget how much her father had hurt her and how much she would be leaving behind when she moved to Austin.

Jack's being there today had made everything ten times worse. All through dinner she'd felt his eyes on her, and she knew he was wondering what was eating her.

Well, let him wonder. Let them all wonder.

None of them *really* cared about her, because if they did, they would have stuck up for her long ago.

By the time Sheila reached her apartment, she had worked herself up to the point where she knew she would spend the rest of the day crying her eyes out.

"Man, Sheila sure was in some kind of snit today," Kevin said. He and Jack were standing in the driveway of Kevin's parents' house watching Scott and Keith shoot baskets.

"Yeah, I noticed that, too. What do you think was wrong?"

Kevin shrugged. "Who knows? Women are a mystery to me. Maybe she had a fight with her boyfriend."

Jack frowned before he could stop himself. "I didn't know she had a boyfriend."

"Hey, I don't know if she does or not. I was just guessing."

"She's your sister. You're supposed to know."

Kevin laughed. "It's clear *you* never had a sister. Believe me, she doesn't tell us stuff like that. She doesn't want us to give her a hard time."

"Well, maybe you should *ask* her. If some guy's giving her a hard time, we'll beat the stuffing out of him."

Kevin gave him a look of disbelief. "Jeez, Jack, lighten up. Believe me, Sheila wouldn't thank us for sticking our noses into her business. She'd be the first to tell you she can take care of herself."

"Maybe *she* thinks so, but I know what guys are like, and so do you."

"What's got into you, anyway? Sheila's fine. It's probably her time of the month, or something."

Jack scowled, but he let the subject drop. But he kept thinking about what Kevin had said, and by the time he left to go home, he'd decided that even though Sheila was off-limits to him, she was fair game to all the other horny guys out there, and *somebody* had to look out for her. So if her brothers weren't going to do it, maybe he'd have to.

The next morning Sheila had the granddaddy of all headaches. The last thing she wanted was to go to work and have another confrontation with her father, but she was determined not to let another day go by without carrying through on her promise to resign.

So on the dot of eight, she unlocked the office and began to get set up for the day. At eight-thirty, her father walked in.

"'Mornin', Sheila."

"'Mornin', Daddy." She busied herself fixing him a cup of coffee the way she did every morning. Black with two sugars.

Normally, he would have walked straight into his office after greeting her. Today he was still standing there when she turned around. She handed him the steaming mug. His eyes met hers. "Sheila, love, I hope you're not still angry with me."

"No, I'm not angry," she answered evenly.

"Good." He smiled, his face relaxing into relieved lines. "I knew you'd come to your senses after a good night's sleep."

She walked over to her desk and reached for the letter she'd typed and printed off only moments before he'd walked through the door. "If you mean you thought I'd change my mind, you were wrong. Here. This is my letter of resignation."

He sighed. "Now, Sheila—"

"Take it, Daddy. Otherwise, I'll just go put it on your desk."

"I'm not taking it. I refuse to accept it."

"Fine. Have it your way. But saying you refuse to accept it won't make any difference. I'm leaving in two weeks. So if you don't want this job to go un*manned,* you'd better start looking for someone to take my place." And with that, she walked into his office and laid the letter in the middle of his desk. Picking up the shamrock-shaped crystal paperweight that had been her birthday gift to him on his last birthday, she anchored the letter by placing it squarely in the middle.

Then, heart beating too fast again, she walked back out to her office and sat down at her computer. She ignored her father.

A long silent moment went by, during which the only sounds were the loud ticking of the wall clock and the click of Sheila's nails against the computer keys. Sheer force of will kept her from turning to look at her father, although she was dying to see the expression on his face.

Finally, still without saying a word, he walked into his office and closed the door.

At ten o'clock, the phone rang.

Sheila picked it up. "Callahan Construction."

"Hi, Sheila. It's Jan."

"Oh, hi, Jan."

"Listen, I know you usually bring a lunch, but I'm dying for some Mexican food. I was wondering, would you like to meet me for lunch?"

Sheila eyed her father's closed office door. "That sounds great. I wouldn't mind getting out of here for a while. What time did you want to go?"

"How about if I pick you up at eleven-thirty? I'm having my yearly well-woman check today at one-thirty, so that should give me enough time."

"Yuck."

"I know. I hate going, but it's a necessary evil."

"The only part I really mind is the Pap smear."

Jan laughed. "Who doesn't?"

A few minutes before eleven-thirty, Sheila knocked on her father's door. She heard what sounded like a grunt, and opened the door a couple of inches. Her father was sitting at his desk studying some plans. "I'm leaving for lunch now."

Patrick didn't look up. "Leave my door open when you go."

"Okay. I'll see you later," she said pleasantly.

Grabbing her purse and windbreaker, she walked outside. She'd barely shut the door behind her when

she spied Jan's Suburban pulling into the lot. Jan circled and stopped in front of the office.

"Hi," she said as Sheila opened the passenger door and hoisted herself up.

"Hi." Sheila reached for the seat belt. She smiled at Jan. She really liked both her sisters-in-law, but she felt closer to Jan because she and Patrick had been married ever since Sheila was a kid and had taken her all kinds of places with them, both before and after they had children of their own. She'd always been able to talk to Jan about things she couldn't tell her mother.

Once they were on their way, Jan said, "I'm glad you could go today. And by the way, Susan's meeting us there."

"Is she? Good. I don't see enough of you two away from those brothers of mine."

Jan smiled. "I know. We need a regular fix of just girl talk."

For the remainder of the ride to the restaurant, they chatted about Jan's girls. Sheila commented that Jana was getting to be a knockout.

"Yes," Jan said, "I'm afraid she is. She's got a boyfriend, you know."

"No. I didn't know. Who is he?"

"Alex Caselli."

"Alex *Caselli?* You mean little Alex that lives next door to Mom and Dad?"

"The very one. Only he isn't so little anymore. I'd say he's at least six feet tall and probably still growing."

"Alex Caselli." Sheila shook her head in amazement. "I can't believe it. Are they *dating?*"

Jan sighed. "Yes, I'm afraid so. We held out as long as we could, but Jana's sixteen. We couldn't keep her from dating forever."

Sheila chuckled. "I'll bet Patrick would have liked to, though."

Jan grinned. "I'm sure he wishes they still had chastity belts. He'd put them on all his daughters."

They both laughed, then Jan's face sobered. "Seriously, it worries me how fast she's growing up. How fast they're *all* growing up."

"I guess all mothers are the same. You sounded just like Mom when you said that."

"I can't help it. It's such a dangerous world. It frightens me to think that in just a couple of years Jana will be out in it, and then two years later, so will Katie."

"You can't protect them forever."

"I know." Jan smiled crookedly. "But I can try." The restaurant was coming up on the right, and Jan turned on her blinker. As they pulled into the parking lot, they saw Susan getting out of her car. She was much more dressed up than either of them in a dark green wool suit worn with bone pumps and matching hose.

"She always looks so nice, doesn't she?" Jan said, ruefully glancing down at her navy corduroy jumper and flat shoes.

"You look just fine," Sheila said. "Look at me. I'm in jeans."

"If I looked the way you do in jeans, I'd wear them, too."

"Oh, for heaven's sake, Jan. You look great in jeans!"

Jan grimaced. "My hips are too big."

Sheila shook her head. "I give up."

By now they'd gotten out of the Suburban and were within hearing distance of Susan.

"Who are you giving up on?" she asked, giving them each a hug.

"This idiot here," Sheila said, indicating Jan. "She thinks her hips are too big."

Susan added her reassurances to Sheila's as the three entered the restaurant. They didn't talk during the flurry of getting seated and giving the waiter their drink orders. But once their chips and salsa were placed on the table and they had their drinks, Jan looked at Sheila and said, "I had an ulterior motive in asking you to come to lunch with us today."

"Oh?" Sheila said, giving first Jan, then Susan a questioning glance.

"Yes," Susan said. "We talked about it after you left the house yesterday, and neither of us think your excuse about cramps is the real reason you wanted to go."

"The thing is," Jan added, "you were acting funny all through dinner. Not like yourself at all."

Well, Sheila guessed, there was no time like the present to tell them her news. She heaved a sigh. "You're right."

"See?" Jan said to Susan. "I *knew* it."

Susan's brown eyes were curious as they met Sheila's. "Want to tell us about it?"

Sheila drank some of her Diet Coke. "Yes. I was upset with Dad yesterday. We had a...disagreement before everyone else showed up."

"Do you mind telling us what about?" Jan asked.

Sheila shrugged. "You'll have to know sooner or later." She explained the ultimatum she'd given her father. "Anyway, he said he would not change his mind. That's what upset me. The fact that he'd rather see me leave Rainbow's End than back down." The hurt she'd managed to submerge most of the morning crept into her voice.

"Oh, Sheila," Jan said, laying a comforting hand over hers. "I'm sorry."

"I'm sorry, too," Susan said.

"But you're not *really* going to leave, are you?" Jan said.

"Yes, I am. I gave Dad my letter of resignation this morning."

"Oh, no!" Jan said. "Sheila, you *can't* leave. I'll miss you too much."

"I'll miss you, too," Susan said, "but I understand how you feel. It's hard when someone else is trying to dictate the way you should live your life."

Sheila knew Susan was remembering when her former mother-in-law had tried to keep her from seeing Keith. "So you don't think I'm crazy the way Dad does?"

Susan shook her head. "No. I don't."

''Susan,'' Jan protested. ''Don't tell her that. I don't want her to go.''

''Well, I don't, either,'' Susan said. ''But I have to be honest. Frankly, Sheila, I don't know how you've stood it all these years. I mean, I love your father, but he's very controlling.''

Sheila nodded glumly. ''That he is. 'Course, he'd never admit it. In his mind, he's just being a good father. Looking out for me.''

''This is awful. I don't want you to go,'' Jan said again.

''Believe me, I don't *want* to go,'' Sheila said. ''I'll miss everyone terribly. But I feel I have no choice. And it won't be so bad. I'll still be close. I can come see you guys on the weekends.''

But even as she said the words, she knew it would be awful. She would hate being away from everything and everyone she loved, and yet, as she'd said, what other choice did she have?

Chapter Three

Jack's cell phone buzzed. Unclipping it from his tool belt, he extended the antenna and pushed the talk button. "Kinsella."

"Hello, Jack."

Funny how just the sound of Old Man Callahan's voice caused Jack to stand straighter. "Hello, Mr. Callahan."

"Just wanted you to know I've called a meeting of all the foremen in my office at five-thirty."

"All right. I'll be there."

"How's everything going there?"

The question surprised Jack. Patrick Callahan was not one for idle chatter, plus he knew if Jack were having any problems at all, Patrick would have been informed promptly. "Everything's going fine," Jack said cautiously.

"No problems with the crew."

"No." Jack was now even more mystified. What was on the old man's mind?

"Let's see. You've got Rick Clemmons, Bobby Roeder and Tony Delgado. Plus the Garcia brothers."

"Yeah. And Frankie Sanders."

"All experienced men."

Jack waited. That something more was coming, he was sure. What that something could be, he had no idea.

"So you wouldn't mind having a rookie to train."

"A rookie to train?"

"Yes. Now that we've got that school job in Pollero, we're going to have to hire more men. And I'm afraid we'll probably have to train them."

Jack nodded, even though Patrick couldn't see him. With the booming economy in this part of Texas, it was getting harder and harder to find experienced workers.

"Anyway, I'm just thinking. No decisions have been made yet. We'll talk about it when the time comes."

After they hung up, Jack turned his attention back to his crew. But the conversation stayed on his mind, especially the reason for the meeting. He wondered what was up. Patrick, Sr. normally called meetings when there was either a big deal in the works or some crisis. Jack hadn't heard of any new big deals—as far as he knew, they weren't even bidding

on anything right now—and he wasn't aware of any crises, either.

At five-thirty he pulled his truck into the office parking lot. Rory's and Kevin's trucks were already there. He noticed that Sheila's car was gone, though. Probably a good thing. He'd been spending way too much time thinking about her lately.

By the time he'd gotten himself a cold drink out of the refrigerator and joined Kevin and Rory in their father's office, Glenn and Keith had arrived. That left only Ed Bassett, a contemporary and former competitor of Patrick, Sr.'s. Patrick had put Ed on the payroll a year earlier when his business had gone bankrupt.

"Ed can't make the meeting," Patrick, Sr. said when the rest of them were seated in his office. "So we'll get started." He handed Patrick, Jr. a piece of paper. "Read this letter and pass it on, son."

Patrick, Jr. began to read. Abruptly, he stopped, raising startled eyes to his father.

His father shrugged. When Patrick, Jr. seemed about to speak, his father said, "Wait. Let them all read it first. Then we'll talk."

Now Jack was *really* curious. As the letter made the rounds, each of the brothers had the same surprised reaction as Patrick, Jr. Finally it was Jack's turn to read the letter. His eyes widened when he realized it was a letter of resignation. And from Sheila!

"So now you know what I wanted to talk to you about," Patrick, Sr. said. He fiddled with his pen.

"What's going on? Why is she quitting?" asked Keith.

"I'm getting to that. She told me what she was planning to do yesterday before y'all got to the house. Actually, when you come right down to it, she threatened me." He grimaced. "I didn't think she really meant it, though." He went on to explain what Sheila had said and what it was she wanted.

Throughout the recital Jack stifled his urge to smile. Sheila had *threatened* her father? He had a feeling this was a first for the old man, who was rarely bucked by anyone. Jack knew he sure would think twice before handing Patrick, Sr. an ultimatum.

"That's our Sheila," muttered Kevin when his father finished. "Fearless."

Jack saw that Rory, too, was trying to cover up the fact that he found the situation amusing. "So what are you gonna do, Dad?" he asked.

"The thing I'm *not* going to do is let her move away."

Wonder how he planned to accomplish that? After all, Sheila was an adult. Plus, Jack couldn't imagine anyone stopping Sheila from doing something she wanted to do.

"How are you going to stop her?" Glenn asked, putting Jack's thoughts into words.

Patrick, Sr. sighed. "I guess I don't have a choice. I'll have to let her go to work on one of the crews."

Rory made a sound like a snort.

Patrick, Sr. glared at Rory. ''What's so all-fired funny about this, Rory?''

''Nothing,'' Rory said innocently.

''Then why are you laughing?''

''Me? I'm not laughing.''

His father's eyes narrowed, but he let the subject drop.

''You know, Dad,'' Kevin said thoughtfully, ''maybe letting her work on a crew isn't such a bad idea. You know yourself how hard the work is, especially in the beginning. Shoot, let her try it. We can give her all the hardest stuff to do. Make it really tough on her. I'll bet it won't take long before she'll be ready to quit without any prompting from us.''

There were enthusiastic murmurs of agreement from everyone but Glenn, who shook his head, saying, ''I don't know, Kevin. She's stubborn. Besides, piling the hardest work on her is not really fair, is it?''

Kevin rolled his eyes.

''I think maybe your brother has the right idea,'' Patrick, Sr. said. ''Yes. I like it.'' His forehead knit in thought. ''Hard work, yes. Enough to show her she doesn't belong out there with a crew. But I don't want her to get hurt.''

''No, no, of course not,'' they all said.

''We just want to teach her a lesson.''

''Yes,'' everyone agreed.

Jack wasn't so sure about any of this. As Glenn had pointed out, Sheila was a stubborn woman. But considering he wasn't part of the family, he'd keep

his mouth shut. If something went wrong with whatever plan they ultimately adopted, he didn't want to be the one they blamed.

Patrick, Sr. studied them all for a long moment. "All right. This is what we'll do. Sheila will begin work in two weeks' time...or longer, if it takes me longer to find someone to replace her in the office. And when she does, she will be assigned to Jack's crew."

Jack stared at him. "*My* crew?"

"Yes. I think it's better if she doesn't work for one of her brothers. And I know you'll keep a sharp eye on her."

"But I—" Even though only yesterday Jack had decided she might need looking after, he certainly had never envisioned anything like this. The last thing he wanted was to be responsible for Sheila working on his construction crew. What if something happened to her? What if she got hurt? He knew who was going to catch the blame for it, and it wouldn't be Sheila. He'd have to watch her like a hawk. And if he was spending most of his time watching out for her, he'd never get anything else done. Yet he knew it would be useless to protest. Once the old man made up his mind about something, that was it. With an inward sigh, he said, "All right, Mr. Callahan. I'll do my best."

As they all filed out of the meeting, Kevin slung an arm over Jack's shoulder.

"Hey, man, it won't be *that* bad having Sheila

working for you. In fact, it might be fun to teach my little sister a lesson or two.''

''Yeah, sure,'' Jack said glumly. ''About as much fun as having a root canal.''

He climbed into his truck with Kevin's laughter still ringing in his ears.

Sheila was surprised to see her father's truck already in the parking lot when she arrived for work the following morning. He wasn't usually at the office this early. Was something wrong? She walked inside to find him sitting on the edge of her desk, mug of coffee in hand. He'd made the coffee, too? That was a first.

''You win, Sheila,'' he said before she had a chance to say anything.

It took her a moment to comprehend what he'd said. But when she did, her heart gave an ecstatic leap. ''I win?'' She hardly dared believe her father had actually changed his mind. ''You mean...?''

Eyeing her gravely, he nodded. ''Yes. I mean I'm going to let you go to work on one of the crews.'' When she whooped, he held up a warning hand. ''But there are two conditions.''

''All right.'' She knew she was grinning like a fool, but she couldn't help it.

''The first is that you stay at this desk until I find a replacement for you.''

''But that could take forever.'' Especially if her father dragged his feet. Was that his plan? He'd never find anyone suitable to replace her?

"Not if we start looking right away. If *you* start looking right away," he amended. "In fact, finding someone to replace you is going to be your responsibility, because you know better than I do what the job entails. You can start by getting an ad in the paper."

Sheila nodded her agreement. She guessed his proviso was justified. "All right. And what's the second condition?"

"When you *do* start working with a crew, there will be no special treatment because you're a woman and especially not because you're my daughter."

"I know that. I don't expect any special treatment."

"Good, because you'll be given the same work to do as any other trainee. If we find someone else from that ad you put in the other day, you'll be trained together."

Sheila smiled. "That's great."

"Now here's the condition...if you can't do the work or if you ever endanger anyone else's life, you'll be terminated. Understand?"

"Yes, of course. The same would be true of any worker, wouldn't it?"

"Yes. But I didn't want you to think an exception would be made for you, because it won't."

"I wouldn't want it any other way." She'd do what was expected if it killed her. "Thank you, Daddy. You won't be sorry. I promise you."

"Huh," he grunted. "I'm sorry already."

Sheila laughed and threw her arms around him. After a moment, he embraced her in return.

As they drew apart, he shook his head. ''I still think this is foolish, love.''

''I know you do, Daddy. But you'll see. I'm going to prove you wrong.''

''I don't want you to think I'm not happy for you, Sheila. It's just that I'm sad for myself. I really wanted us to move to Austin.''

''I know you did, and I'm sorry, Carrie.'' Sheila had called Carrie the minute she got home to tell her the news.

Carrie sighed. ''Oh, well...''

''You could still move.'' Carrie was a dental technician—a really good one—and could get a great job anywhere.

''I know. I'll think about it.''

They both knew she wouldn't. Sometimes Sheila wondered why the two of them had stayed friends for so long. They were so totally different. But maybe, like Sheila and Glenn, their differences were what kept their relationship interesting.

''So now you have to find your own replacement, huh?'' Carrie said.

''Yep.''

''Gee, in a way I wish I had office skills. I wouldn't mind working there.''

''What? Since when? I thought you loved what you do.''

''I do love what I do, but, well...''

"Well, what?"

"Well, it would be fun to be around all those guys."

"Carrie, sweetie, I hate to burst your bubble, but I don't get to see that many guys. They don't come into the office unless they have to, and that usually means it's payday or they're sick and need forms or something. Otherwise, they're on site somewhere. Anyway, it's a myth that construction workers are sexy. Mostly, they're just dirty and smelly." Liar. What about Jack? You think *he's* sexy.

"Some of them are sexy no matter how dirty they are," Carrie pointed out.

Sheila had known for a long time that Carrie had a crush on Glenn. Unfortunately, it was a crush that would never go anywhere, because Sheila—unbeknownst to Carrie—had already sounded Glenn out on the topic, and he'd bluntly said he wasn't interested. "I know she's a good friend," he'd told her, "and nice and all that, but she's not my type."

"Well, you don't have office skills. Besides, you make more money doing what you do." Sheila felt bad that she always steered their conversation in another direction when Carrie started dropping hints about Glenn, but what else could she do? She didn't want to hurt Carrie's feelings by telling her the truth, and she would have to if Carrie ever got bold enough to suggest that Sheila might do some matchmaking. "And you have flexibility, too." Carrie only worked four days a week.

Carrie sighed again. "True."

"Anyway, enough of that," Sheila said. "Tell me about Claudia's wedding. Did you guys find dresses on Saturday?"

Soon Carrie was happily describing her sister's upcoming wedding and the topic of the construction office was dropped.

Later that night, Sheila thought about their conversation again. She'd just finished writing the ad she would place the next day, and she remembered the wistful note in Carrie's voice when she'd talked about being around the guys. Sheila hoped the women who responded to the ad weren't all going to have Carrie's mistaken impression about the job, because there was nothing glamorous about it.

However, that wasn't her concern. All she cared about was finding a qualified person to take her place. She smiled happily. And the sooner, the better.

By the following Monday Sheila was mighty worried. They'd run their ad for an office manager for the past five days, and so far, of the seven people who had responded, none had the qualifications or experience they were looking for. If Sheila hadn't talked to the respondents personally, she might have thought her father *was* dragging his feet, but she *had* talked to them, and in good conscience, she had to admit none was worth bringing in for an interview.

Darn. At this rate she'd be working in the office for years. Maybe they should look farther afield. She decided she would call Susan at the community col-

lege to see if she had any suggestions. Just as she reached for the phone, it rang.

"Callahan Construction."

"Yes. I'm calling about the ad for an office manager," said a pleasant female voice.

"Why, yes," Sheila said enthusiastically, crossing her fingers. "I'm Sheila Callahan. I'm the one who placed the ad."

"Hello, Miss Callahan. My name is Justine Edmund, and I'm very interested in the position."

"Tell me about yourself." If Sheila could have crossed her toes, she would have.

"Well, I'm a single mother of fourteen-year-old twin girls. I have an associate degree in accounting from Austin Community College, and for the past five years I've been working at the hospital in the accounting department."

"Are you still employed there?"

"No. I quit last month."

"May I ask why?"

After a slight hesitation, the Edmund woman said, "I hope you won't hold this against me, because I'm going to tell you the truth. I simply could not work another day for the man who was my supervisor. I am not a hard person to get along with, Miss Callahan. In fact, I feel I deal with people very well, but this man was impossible. I think he is insecure and felt threatened by my capabilities and skills. At any rate, he made my life a living hell, and it was affecting my health. So I quit."

"And you've been looking for a job ever since?"

"No. I decided I deserved some time off, so I've been catching up on things around the house and just relaxing and enjoying life. But now I'm ready to go back to work. I *need* to go back to work. And the position you advertised sounded perfect."

"You do know it's a one-person office?"

"Yes, that's what appeals to me most. Being in charge. Not having to worry about stepping on someone else's toes. Not having to deal with somebody's fragile ego. Plus, there would be a variety of work."

So far Sheila really liked this woman's answers. She mentally crossed her fingers. "Are you available to come in and talk to me this afternoon?"

"Certainly. What time?"

They set up the interview for three o'clock. Sheila told her where they were located, told her to be sure and bring a copy of her résumé, and then they hung up. Sheila closed her eyes and sent a silent prayer heavenward.

Justine Edmund turned out to be a tall, attractive redhead with a nice smile and completely professional manner. Her résumé was impressive. Before her divorce, she'd lived and worked in Austin, holding down the same position for ten years, with a steady progression of duties and earnings.

When Sheila talked about the responsibilities she'd have at Callahan Construction, Justine made intelligent, informed comments and asked incisive, educated questions.

When asked, she unhesitatingly gave Sheila the

names of her former supervisors, even the one she'd quit her hospital job to get away from.

"I don't think he'll lie about me," she said. "He'd be too afraid I'd sue him."

By the time the interview was over at four o'clock, Sheila knew that if Justine Edmund's references checked out, the job would be hers. And she said as much. "You'll have to meet my dad before we can make any kind of formal offer, but I don't think he'll have any objections."

Sheila was rewarded with a big smile and unmistakable relief in the other woman's eyes.

"Thank you," Justine said, rising. "I think I'd really like working here, and the job would be an answer to a prayer. I was afraid, because there aren't that many good jobs here in Rainbow's End, that I might have to move back to Austin. I wouldn't mind so much, but the girls are so happy here. They love the high school. They're on the drill team and Monica's on the debate team and Melanie was elected class treasurer. They'd be heartbroken if we had to move."

The minute Justine was out the door, Sheila got busy calling her references. Justine had been right. All three former supervisors gave her glowing reports, even the most recent one. He did have one caveat.

"I'll warn you," he said, "she's smart and capable and all that, but she's stubborn. She always thinks her way is best."

She sounded more perfect all the time, Sheila

thought in amusement. After concluding the call, she headed into her father's office to tell him their search was over.

Justine Edmund started to work two days later. Within a week, there was nothing left for Sheila to show her. In fact, Justine had already come up with ideas on how to revamp the filing system and how to simplify the way they ordered supplies.

In the process, they had become friends. Sheila told Justine all about her family and her excitement about her new job. Surprising herself, she even told Justine about Jack and her feelings for him.

"I can't believe he doesn't notice you as a woman," Justine said. "Are you sure he's not blind?"

Sheila grimaced. "No, he's not blind. He just thinks of me as a kid—my brothers' little sister—the way he always has."

On Sheila's last day—a Friday and payday—Justine got to meet Jack when he came in for his paycheck.

He gave her his cocky smile and shook her hand. "It's nice to meet you, Justine."

"You, too, Jack."

"So, Sheila," he said, turning to her. "I guess you'll be starting to work for me on Monday."

She nearly choked. "For *you?*"

"Didn't your father tell you? You've been assigned to my crew."

Oh, my God. "No, he didn't tell me."

"You won't be alone. We have another recruit starting Monday, too. Kenny Romero. Have you met him?"

Sheila nodded, still stunned by the information that she'd be working for Jack. "He came in to fill out his paperwork yesterday," she murmured.

"Good. I'll tell you what I told him. My crew will be out at Willowbend for at least six months. Well, you knew that."

Sheila nodded.

"So on Monday report to the Willowbend site at seven-thirty."

"Wh-what about tools and things?" Sheila was still trying to come to terms with the fact that she'd be working on Jack's crew.

"You won't need tools for what you'll be doing to begin with."

Was it Sheila's imagination, or did Jack's smile seem crafty?

"Nice to meet you, Justine," he said. He gave them a parting smile, then left.

When the door shut behind him, Justine said, "I can see why you feel the way you do. He's a very attractive man."

"And he knows it," Sheila said glumly.

"What's wrong?" Justine said. "I'd've thought you'd be overjoyed that you're going to be in such close proximity to him. A dream come true."

Sheila shook her head. "No. It'll be bad enough that I have to learn the job and prove I can do it as well as any of the guys, but to have to be around

Jack the whole time, too, well...'' She ran her fingers through her hair in frustration. ''It's going to be torture.''

''You don't want your old job back, do you?'' Justine said in alarm.

Sheila grinned ruefully. ''It's too late for that.'' For a moment, she was frightened and wished she could turn back the clock. But the fear didn't last long. She could do this. She could do anything. She straightened her shoulders. ''You know what? You're right. It *is* a dream come true. I'm going to be doing what I've always wanted to do, and who knows? Maybe I'll end up teaching Jack Kinsella a thing or two in the process.''

Sheila spent the day Saturday looking for a good pair of work boots. She'd been around construction workers long enough to know she needed a well-made, sturdy pair. She met Carrie for a late lunch, then they decided to drive into Austin to hit the music scene.

On Sunday, she wished she could skip the family dinner. She wasn't in the mood to put up with a lot of teasing about her new job, and she was sure her father wouldn't appreciate it, either. But surprisingly, even when Keith said, ''So tomorrow's the big day, huh?'' the rest of them didn't pick up on it.

Soon after, something happened that wiped even Sheila's mind clear of her new job. They had just

said grace and begun to pass the food when Keith tapped his spoon against his water glass.

"Susan and I have something we want to tell you," he said.

They exchanged a look so filled with love it hurt Sheila to see it, because it made her agonizingly aware that although she had accomplished her goal regarding her job, there was still something vital missing from her own life.

Keith reached for Susan's hand. "In six months, we're going to be giving Scott and Megan a sister or brother."

A chorus of ohs and ahs greeted the announcement, and for the rest of the dinner, the coming grandchild was all anyone could talk about.

"I'm so happy for you, Susan," Sheila said when dinner was over and the two of them, along with Jan and her older girls, were helping with cleanup.

"We all are," Jan added.

"We all are what?"

Everyone turned as Glenn entered the kitchen.

"Happy for Susan and Keith," Jan said.

Glenn smiled at Susan. "Yeah, it's cool about the baby." He turned to Sheila. "Can we talk for a minute?"

"Sure. What's up?"

He inclined his head toward the back door. "Let's go out back."

Giving her sisters-in-law a mystified look, Sheila followed Glenn out the door.

Once outside, he said, "Listen, I've been thinking about something and I decided I'd better warn you."

"Warn me?"

"Yeah." He kicked at a loose pebble. "Tomorrow? They're gonna give you a hard time."

"On the job, you mean?"

He nodded.

Sheila grinned. "Tell me something I *don't* know, Glenn."

"Thing is, it's gonna be real tough. I just wanted you to be prepared."

"Oh, I'm prepared. What? Are they going to try to scare me off? Is that it?"

He nodded again.

"Let 'em try. I don't scare easy."

His eyes, that same electrifying blue of all her brothers, finally met hers. "You know, I really wish you'd forget about this, Sheila. 'Cause Dad's right. A construction crew is no place for a woman. You have no idea how rough it can get."

"I don't care. I want this, and I'm not going to forget about it."

He sighed. "You sure are stubborn."

She grinned. "Yes, I am."

"Well, if you're determined to go through with this, let me give you some hints. Bring some heavy gloves and be sure to wear something that covers up your arms so you don't get sunburned. Better yet, put on a good sunscreen. Oh, and wear a hat with a brim."

Sheila frowned. "But won't I wear a hard hat?"

"Not tomorrow. Probably not for a couple of weeks."

"Why not?"

"Because tomorrow you're going to do what all the inexperienced guys do the first day on the job. First you'll set forms, then you'll dig trenches."

Sheila grimaced over the digging part, but she knew Glenn was right, because she'd heard other new hires talk about having to do the grunt work when they first started. And her father had said they weren't going to give her special treatment.

"Thanks, Glenn. I knew about the sunscreen, but I hadn't thought about bringing gloves."

He put his arm around her as they walked back to the house. "Good luck tomorrow."

She smiled.

"And Sheila, if things get too tough—"

"They won't."

"I know. But if they *do,* there's no shame in admitting you might have made a mistake."

Reaching up, she kissed him on the cheek. "You're sweet to worry about me, Glenn, but you don't have to. This isn't a mistake. I've wanted this for years, and it's all going to work out just fine. You'll see."

Chapter Four

Knowing what you were going to have to do and actually doing it were two distinctly different things, Sheila decided wearily. She put her right foot on the shoulder of the shovel for what seemed like the thousandth time that day and, grunting, bore down with all her weight.

Sweat had long ago soaked through the T-shirt she had started out wearing under a long-sleeved flannel shirt. The flannel shirt had bitten the dust about noon. It was now three-thirty, and if there was still a God up there in heaven, she could drag her exhausted body home in thirty minutes.

"Man, I'm beat," Kenny Romero said. "I work out and all, but I wasn't prepared for this."

"I know." She and Kenny had been digging this trench for hours.

"How many days you think we're gonna have to do this?"

Sheila shrugged. "I don't know." Kenny was a sweet guy, but she was too tired to talk. In fact, she wasn't sure she could still walk. If she felt this bad today, she couldn't imagine how she would feel tomorrow.

And to think she'd been so excited this morning. So eager to begin work. Actually, what they'd done the first few hours of the day hadn't been that bad. Jack had started her and Kenny with setting forms: putting stakes in the ground around the perimeter of the house they were starting to build. After they'd finished driving in the stakes, he had shown them how to connect each stake with string—ending with an accurate outline of the house.

It was what came next that was the killer: digging the trenches that would hold the form boards that would in turn be the base for the concrete foundation. Backbreaking labor, that's what it was. Sheila couldn't believe the crews still did this work by hand. Couldn't they buy a backhoe or something?

Thank God they were nearly finished—for this house, anyway—although their company was building dozens of houses in this development. She was also thankful that she'd managed to get through the day without complaining, even though the work was harder than anything she had ever done—certainly no workout had ever compared—and her body was crying out for rest. But Sheila had called on reserves of strength she hadn't known she possessed to make

sure she matched Kenny shovelful for shovelful. She knew Jack was watching her, and at the slightest sign that she couldn't hold her own, he'd have something to say. Worse, he'd have something negative to report to her father.

There was no way she'd give him the opportunity. She'd rather die first. *Maybe I will die, but I'll wait until I'm home and he can't see me.*

Finally it was four o'clock and Jack told the crew they could leave for the day if they wanted to.

If they wanted to?

Sheila groaned inwardly. She knew what that meant. That meant they were under budget and Jack had the authority to grant overtime to anyone who desired it. Would he take it as a sign of what he would be sure to term typical female weakness if she quit for the day instead of grabbing the extra pay the way a lot of the guys would?

While she was debating what to do, he walked over to the site where she and Kenny labored. Sheila forced herself to keep digging.

"You two can knock off for the day," he said.

Kenny immediately dropped his shovel and raised his eyes heavenward. "Thank you, Lord."

"Don't forget to put the shovel in the equipment shed," Jack directed.

"I'm goin' right now," Kenny said.

Sheila finally looked up, resting her arms on the handle of her shovel. Jack's hazel eyes—even shaded as they were by his hard hat—held a gleam of something softer than she'd expected. If she

hadn't known better, she'd almost have thought he felt sorry for her.

"If you need me to stay longer, I can," she said.

She could see he was holding back a smile.

"I appreciate the offer, but you've both done enough for the first day."

"Don't argue with the man, Sheila," Kenny said, his dark eyes giving her an are-you-crazy? look.

Now Jack did smile. "Telling Sheila not to argue is like telling the sun not to shine."

Kenny laughed, but Sheila didn't think Jack's comment was funny. She wanted to say so, but she didn't have the energy. And although she would never let Jack know it, she was grateful she could now go home and lick her wounds.

"Fine." She walked over to where she'd thrown her flannel shirt and picked it up. "See you tomorrow then." Trying not to grimace, she started to follow Kenny to the equipment truck.

"Sheila, wait."

She stopped and slowly turned around.

"Ben-Gay will help."

She started to say she didn't need his sympathy or his help. But something in his expression stopped her. "Thanks."

He smiled. "See you tomorrow."

She had guts. He'd give her that.

Jack watched as Sheila walked away from him. He knew she was trying hard to walk normally, even though he was sure every muscle in her body was

screaming in protest. It was a long time ago that he'd put in his first day on the job, but he still remembered how miserable he was afterward. How all he'd wanted to do at the end of that day was crawl home and collapse on the bed.

But even exhausted, sweaty and dirty, Sheila still managed to look sexy. Her jeans hugged every curve in her body, and that T-shirt she was wearing left little to the imagination. He wondered if she had any idea how sexy she looked. The men sure had noticed.

In fact, right now two of the ones who were supposed to be working overtime were staring after her. He walked toward them. "What're you two looking at?" His voice was deceptively soft.

Bobby Roeder, who'd worked under Jack the longest, gave a low whistle. "Nice piece of—"

"Watch your mouth, Roeder," Jack said, cutting him off. "And keep your eyes where they belong."

"Ah, heck, Jack," Bobby said. "I'm just lookin', that's all. There ain't no harm in that. You gotta admit, she's a good-lookin' babe."

Jack felt like punching that stupid grin off Bobby's face, but good sense prevailed. "Keep your eyes where they belong," he bit out. "That's the boss's daughter. And don't you forget it."

And he'd better not forget it, either.

The first thing Sheila did when she got home was turn on the shower as hot as she thought she could stand it. Then she stripped off her clothes and stood

under the spray for a long time. When she finally emerged, the only thing she had strength enough left to do was drink a glass of milk and fall into bed.

Hours later, she awakened to the insistent ringing of the phone next to her ear. "'Lo," she mumbled.

"Sheila?"

"Umph."

"Sheila, is that you?"

Sheila groaned as she shifted her weight and tried to open her eyes. There wasn't a single part of her body that didn't hurt. "Yes, it's me." She had finally recognized the voice as belonging to Jan.

"What's wrong? You sound terrible."

"Well, for one thing, I hurt. Plus, I was sleeping. It took me a few minutes to come awake."

"Oh, Sheila, I'm sorry. I forgot. You started work on the crew today. I take it it was bad."

"You could say that."

"Well, listen, in that case, I'll let you get back to sleep."

Sheila's stomach rumbled. "No, that's all right. I'm hungry, anyway." She squinted at the clock. "No wonder. It's after nine."

"Do you want to go get something to eat and maybe call me back later?"

"No. We can talk now. What's up?"

"Are you sure?"

"Jan!"

Jan laughed. "Sorry. I guess I'm so used to mothering people, I can't stop."

Feigning impatience, Sheila said, "Are you gonna tell me why you called or do I have to guess?"

"I'm going to tell you. Remember when I mentioned I was going to the doctor for my physical?"

"Sure. That was the day I gave my notice."

"Well, while I was there Dr. Rodriguez set me up for a mammogram."

Everything in Sheila went still. "Why? Did she find a lump or something?"

"No. She just said at my age I should start having one every year."

Sheila let out the breath she wasn't even aware she was holding. "Oh. God, you scared me for a minute."

"Actually," Jan said slowly, "I, um, had the mammogram Friday, and, um, the radiologist saw a funny spot...something they didn't like, and...well, I'm having a needle biopsy tomorrow. I-I just wanted you to know."

"Jan!" Sheila's aches and pains were forgotten as she swung her legs out of bed and stood, the portable phone clutched to her ear. "Of course you needed to let me know! Where are you having the biopsy? At Tri-City General?"

"Yes."

"What time?"

"Ten in the morning."

"You're not going to be by yourself, are you?" For the first time since she'd started work, Sheila wished she still had her office job, because then she could have taken the morning off to be with Jan. As

it was, she knew she couldn't ask for time off. That would smack of expecting special treatment.

"No, Patrick's taking the day off."

"Good. Listen, Jan, don't worry about this. They just do needle biopsies to be sure everything is okay. It's strictly routine, which I'm sure they've told you."

"Yes, I know."

But Jan's tone told Sheila she *was* worried. Well, of course she was! If Sheila were in her shoes, she'd be worried, too. Any woman would. "Darn. I wish I could be there with you."

"Thanks. I appreciate that. But it's really not necessary."

"I know, but I still wish I could be there." Damn. Maybe she *should* ask for the morning off. After all, what was more important? Jan? Or Sheila's pride? "You know, on second thought, I'll see if I can't get the morning off and come, too."

"No, Sheila, I don't want you to do that. You just started working on the crew, and I know how much it means to you to succeed. This is no big deal tomorrow, really. I don't even know why I called you."

"You called because we're friends. I would have been hurt if you hadn't."

Sheila could almost feel Jan's smile on the other end of the phone. They talked for a while more, with Sheila giving Jan repeated assurances.

But after they hung up, Sheila admitted to herself that she was frightened. What if everything *wasn't*

okay? Jan's mother had died of breast cancer, and Sheila knew that fact alone would make Jan scared to death.

Please God, she prayed. *Don't let this be anything. Jan doesn't deserve to have anything bad happen to her.*

But even as Sheila prayed, she remembered how she used to rail at fate when she was a kid, saying such and such wasn't fair. Her mother always smiled indulgently and told her that nothing about life was fair, and the wise person kept that in mind and didn't waste her energy crying about things she couldn't control or change.

Bad things did happen to good people. All you had to do was read the paper or watch the news to see the proof of that every day.

But not Jan. If I just think positive, everything will be fine. Everything will be fine.

Repeating the words like a mantra, Sheila headed for the kitchen to make herself something to eat.

"I hurt so bad last night I could hardly move," Kenny said the following morning when he and Sheila were taking a break. They were sitting drinking coffee on the tailgate of Kenny's truck and trying to talk over the country music blaring from a co-worker's boom box.

"Tell me about it," Sheila said. She winced. "If anything, I might hurt worse today." Her hands were covered with blisters, too. This morning she'd slathered ointment on them, then put on a pair of

white cotton gloves, which she was wearing under her heavier workmen's gloves. She hoped it helped, but they were still digging trenches, so she had a feeling her precautions might not make any difference.

"Sheila, can I ask you something?"

"Sure." She finished her coffee, wiped out the cup with a tissue, then replaced it on her thermos. Tomorrow she would bring bottled water instead of coffee, she decided, even though the mornings were really cool now and the coffee tasted good.

"What's a girl like you doing working a job like this? I mean, you don't have to do this. You're the old man's daughter."

Sheila sighed. "Jeez, Kenny, don't *you* start." She explained how she hated being cooped up in an office, how she wanted to be a real part of the business like her brothers, and how she'd had to fight for the chance.

Kenny shook his head. "I guess I understand what you're saying, but it doesn't make sense to me. Shoot, I wish I had some kind of skill like you do where I could work in an office and do better for myself."

Sheila shrugged. "People are different."

"Yeah, maybe, but I can't help it. I have to agree with your father and your brothers. This really isn't a good place for a woman." He hesitated. "I mean, most of these guys, they're pretty crude. They been just about poppin' their eyes out starin' at you."

She grimaced. "I know." In fact, she'd decided

this morning that no matter how comfortable T-shirts were, she'd better invest in some cotton work shirts.

"'Course, I can't blame 'em," Kenny added. His dark eyes twinkled. "You're a good-lookin' woman."

"Why, Kenny," Sheila said, "are you flirting with me?" If it had been any of the other guys—excepting Jack, of course—Sheila would have put him in his place real quick. But Kenny was a nice guy. Plus, he was cute, with those dark eyes and that great smile. He kind of reminded her of that young detective on *Law and Order.*

Kenny grinned. "Maybe I am." He hopped down from the tailgate, then reached up to give her a hand. "Break's over."

"Yeah, I know," she said, looking at her watch.

As they headed back to their digging, and Sheila was no longer distracted by conversation with Kenny, her thoughts went back to Jan—where they'd been ever since her call the night before. It was ten-thirty. Was the biopsy over? Was everything all right? She had decided earlier that instead of staying on site to eat the lunch she'd brought, she'd drive over to the office and try to call Patrick. She knew she could ask Jack if she could use the phone in the trailer, but the rule was no phone calls for the crew unless it was an emergency. Checking on Jan really didn't fall into the category of an emergency, so if Jack let her use the trailer phone it would con-

stitute special treatment, something Sheila was determined to avoid at all costs.

It seemed to take forever before the crew knocked off for lunch, but when she checked her watch it was only eleven-thirty. Sheila headed straight for her car.

"You leaving us?"

She whipped around to find Jack walking behind her.

"Don't worry. I'll be back at noon."

He gave her his lazy smile. "And here I thought maybe you were conceding defeat."

"Hah. That'll be the day."

His smile widened. "Did you take my advice about the Ben-Gay?"

Instead of the sharp retort she wanted to make, she said, "Listen, I only have—" She checked her watch. "Twenty-eight minutes left of my lunch break, and I've got something I need to do, so much as I'd like to trade insults, I've gotta go."

She drove away with him standing there watching her, that infuriatingly cocky smile still on his face. One of these days, she decided, she would have the last laugh. One of these days even Jack would have to admit he'd been wrong about her. Because although she might never have Jack in the way she wanted him, she was determined that, at the very least, she would have his respect in terms of her job.

It was too bad, Jack thought. Really too bad that Sheila was off-limits to him, because she was ex-

actly the kind of woman he enjoyed being around—the kind who gave as good as she got. The kind who played it completely straight. You always knew where you stood with Sheila. Every emotion she felt was on her face, and every thought in her head found its way out of her mouth.

That mouth of hers was going to get her in trouble one of these days, in more ways than one. Because in addition to saying exactly what she thought, she had the most kissable lips he'd ever seen.

He remembered reading about somebody's "bee-stung" lips once, and thinking how corny it was. Hell, it might be corny, but it sure described Sheila's delicious-looking mouth.

Jack let his thoughts dwell for a few minutes on how much he'd like to test his theory about Sheila's lips and their kissability quotient. In fact, he was so lost in his pleasant thoughts that he narrowly missed walking into the path of a cement truck. The truck driver blasted his horn, and Jack jumped out of the way.

"Jeez, Jack, watch where you're goin'," the driver yelled. "You coulda been killed."

Jack gave him a rueful smile and decided he'd do well to remember that thoughts of Sheila could be just as dangerous as the lady herself.

"Sheila, hi," said Justine as Sheila walked into the office. "Is something wrong?"

"No, not really. I just needed to use the phone. Mind if I wash up a little first?"

"No, of course not."

Once Sheila had cleaned up, she came back out and picked up the phone. After several unsuccessful tries, she finally located Patrick at the hospital. "I couldn't wait," she said. "How's Jan?"

"The news isn't good," he said in a strained voice.

Sheila swallowed. "Tell me."

Matter-of-factly, he explained that the biopsy had shown a malignancy. "I'm just waiting for her to be released, and tomorrow morning I'm taking her into Austin. Dr. Rodriguez has referred us to a well-known breast surgeon who is also an oncologist. He'll let us know all the options available, and then we'll decide what to do."

"Oh, God, Patrick." Sheila's eyes filled with tears. "I'm so sorry." How insignificant her problems were compared to Jan's and Patrick's. "Do Mom and Dad know?"

"I called Mom about thirty minutes ago. I—I haven't told Dad yet." His voice cracked.

Sheila's eyes met Justine's, who had been trying to pretend she wasn't listening. Holding her hand over the mouthpiece, Sheila inclined her head toward her father's closed office door. "Is he in?"

"No," Justine said.

"Patrick," Sheila said, "I was going to offer to tell Dad for you, but Justine says he's not here right now."

"That's okay." Patrick had obviously regained his control, for his voice was back to normal. "Mom

will tell him. She's on her way to the house in case the kids get home from school before we get there."

Sheila had forgotten all about the girls. Her heart ached for Patrick, who would have the job of telling them, but would have to be careful not to tell them too much, for she was certain he would not want to alarm them unnecessarily. "All right. Well, listen, tell Jan I called and that I'm thinking about her, and I'll call you as soon as I get home tonight, okay?"

"Okay."

When they hung up, Justine gave Sheila a sympathetic look. "Is everything okay?"

"I hope so." Sheila knew Justine was dying to know what was going on, but she didn't feel it was her place to talk about it. "I'd tell you if I could, but—"

"No, no," Justine said. "Don't explain. I just...well, you looked so sad."

Sheila tried to smile, but it was a halfhearted attempt at best. "Thanks for being concerned." She glanced at the clock. "Oh, oh. I'd better get going. My lunch break's nearly over."

Sheila had eaten half a tuna salad sandwich while driving over to the office with the intention of finishing it on the way back to the site. After the conversation with Patrick, though, she'd lost her appetite, but knew she'd better finish her lunch because she'd need the energy to get through the afternoon. So she wolfed down the second half of the sandwich, then started on a Granny Smith apple.

Worry about Jan caused the food to sit like a lump

in her stomach for the rest of the day. The only good thing about her preoccupation with Jan was it took Sheila's mind off her aching muscles and sore back. She could already tell she was going to feel worse tomorrow than she had today. She guessed this would be true until her body finally got used to the work.

"Isn't it time to quit yet?" Kenny groaned at one point. But he said the words under his breath, because he was as determined as she was.

When four o'clock finally rolled around, Jack walked over to where she and Kenny were just finishing up.

"Still here, huh?" The remark was directed at both of them, but his eyes were on Sheila.

"And I'll be here tomorrow," she said.

"Me, too," Kenny added.

"And the day after that," Sheila said. She stripped off her gloves and reached into her jeans' pocket for a tissue, which she used to wipe off her face.

Jack looked at Kenny. "She's tough. Can't scare her off easily."

"You can't scare me off at all."

"That sounds like a dare. Don't you think so?" Again, his remark was directed to Kenny.

Kenny shrugged. "Leave me out of this."

"Take it any old way you like," Sheila said, knowing she should keep quiet. But this was not a day to mess with her.

Jack grinned. ''Okay, tiger. You can have the last word. For now, anyway.''

The exchange had taken Sheila's mind off Jan, but the respite was temporary, for the moment she climbed in her car and headed for home, all other thoughts were wiped from her mind—even Jack and his taunting smile.

As soon as she reached her apartment, she called Patrick's house. Her mother answered the phone.

''Hi, Mom. Are Patrick and Jan home yet?''

''Yes. They got here about an hour ago.''

''How are they doing?''

Her mother lowered her voice. ''All right. They're talking to Jana right now.''

Sheila closed her eyes. ''Oh, Mom.''

''I know. I know.'' Rose's voice broke.

''I feel so bad for them. Do...do they have any idea what's going to happen? Will she have to have a mastectomy?''

''I don't know.''

Sheila sighed. ''Listen, I just got home, and I'm filthy. I'm going to shower and put on some clean clothes, then I'm coming over.''

An hour later, she pulled into the driveway of Jan and Patrick's sprawling ranch-style house on the west side of town—the area where most of the younger families lived. She parked in front and walked up the front walk, admiring the fall chrysanthemums Jan had planted on either side of the front door. Sheila was envious of Jan's green thumb. Sheila couldn't even keep ivy growing in a pot.

God, she thought as she knocked on the front door, then let herself in. This, this *thing* that had happened to Jan was so unfair. She just didn't deserve it.

''Hello,'' she called.

From the back of the house, her mother answered, saying, ''Back here, Sheila.''

Sheila headed for the kitchen, where she found her mother making a salad. Sheila gave her mother a hug, then said, ''Where *is* everybody?''

''Patrick took Jan to Wal-Mart. She wanted to get a few things to take to the hospital with her.''

''The hospital? I thought they were just going to see a specialist?''

''They are, but when Jan's doctor called to make the appointment, they were told she would probably receive her treatment at Seton Medical Center and to be prepared for her to be admitted immediately.''

Sheila knew her eyes held the same alarm and fear she saw reflected in her mother's. She licked her lips. ''That doesn't sound good.''

Rose shook her head. ''No, it doesn't.''

''Wh-where are the girls?''

''Allene and Briana are next door playing with Shannon. Katie's at band practice, and Jana's in her room.'' Her mother's eyes were filled with worry.

''Is Jana upset?''

Rose nodded.

''Poor kid. Do the others know?''

''No. They plan to tell Katie, but Patrick thinks Briana and Allene are too young to spell it all out.''

"What does Jan think?"

"She wants to tell Briana."

"I agree with her. After all, Briana's twelve. That's old enough to understand and give her mother some emotional support."

"I know you mean well, Sheila, but don't say anything about this, okay? Whether they tell the younger girls is Jan's and Patrick's decision, not yours."

Sheila sighed. "Okay. I'm sure you're right."

Her mother smiled and gave her a shoulder hug. "Honey, why don't you go back and talk to Jana? She looks up to you, and I think you can help her."

"I'm not sure I know what to say."

"You'll know what to say."

Sheila nodded. She wished she had her mother's confidence. Thing was, Sheila had never been through anything like this before. All she really knew about breast cancer was what she'd read and the little bit Jan had told her when they'd discussed Jan's mother.

Heart filled with trepidation, she headed for Jana's room.

Chapter Five

Jack stayed at the site until the light was gone, then gathered up the last of the equipment and locked up. On the way home, he stopped at the Kroger near his apartment, where he quickly filled up his basket with enough food and supplies to keep him from having to shop again for a couple of weeks.

When he got to his apartment, he put everything away, then took a fast shower. Barefoot and wearing clean sweats, he headed for the kitchen where he unearthed a cold can of beer. Then he turned on the oven to preheat the broiler. Nursing his beer, he set about trimming and seasoning the pork chops he'd purchased for tonight's dinner.

In the middle of his preparations, the phone rang. Figuring it was just some sales type—they always

seemed to choose the dinner hour to call—he ignored it. "Let the answering machine pick it up," he muttered. But recognizing Kevin's voice, he wiped his hands on a dish towel and grabbed the phone.

"Hey, man, what's goin' on?" Kevin said.

"Just fixing my dinner."

"Well, that settles that. I thought you might want to hit My Amigos for dinner."

"Sorry."

"That's okay. I'll call Rory or Glenn. See if either one of them wants to go. Unless, of course, you want to invite me over to share your dinner. What're you having, anyway?"

"Pork chops. But I didn't buy enough to share."

"I was only kidding. Say, how's it going with Sheila?"

"Not too bad. I haven't had to spend much time watching her because there's nothing to watch when you've got 'em digging trenches. Anyway, you gotta give her credit. She's hanging in there."

"Well, I had my doubts this plan would work, anyway."

"What do you mean, you had your doubts? You're the one who suggested it."

"I know." Kevin chuckled. "I figured, what the hell. If she wanted the job so bad, why not give it to her? But you know how my dad is. I thought it might make it easier for him to swallow the fact that she'd bested him if he believed she'd eventually

throw in the towel and admit she couldn't do the work.''

Jack shook his head. ''You sure had *me* fooled.''

''Besides, I knew whichever one of us she was assigned to wasn't going to be too rough on her. Hell, we like to tease her and give her a hard time, but she *is* our sister.''

''She's not *my* sister,'' Jack pointed out.

''No, but I knew if you got her, you'd be the least hard on her of any of us.''

Jack stiffened. ''What's that supposed to mean?''

''Oh, come on, Jack. You've always had a soft spot for Sheila. I know that.''

''I have not!''

''I don't mean you're hot for her or anything, I just mean you think of her the same way we do, like a kid sister you've got to look out for.''

''Well, sure. Of course, I do.'' Jack expelled his breath in relief. For a minute there, he'd thought Kevin was a mind reader.

''Anyway, I'm glad to hear she's doing okay. I actually hope she makes it, even though I'd never let her know I feel that way. I mean, how many people have ever gotten the best of my father?'' His voice was tinged with amusement.

Jack grinned. ''None that I know of.''

They talked a few more minutes, then Kevin said, ''Before we hang up, there's something else I wanted to talk to you about.''

''Oh?''

''Yeah. I thought you'd want to know. Patrick is

taking Jan into Austin tomorrow morning. To the medical center."

"Is something wrong?"

"Yeah. It's breast cancer."

"Oh, man. That's tough."

"Yeah, it is. Her mother died of it."

Jack swallowed. God.

"Anyway, the family's all torn up about it, Sheila probably more than anyone. She and Jan are tight."

Jack nodded absently. He'd seen the two women together enough to figure as much.

"So you might want to cut Sheila some slack in the next few days."

"Yeah. Listen, thanks for telling me."

After they hung up, Jack stood staring into space. He thought about Jan. How energetic she was. How cheerful. How nice. She was the kind of woman everyone liked, both men and other women. Hell, you couldn't help but like her. She didn't have a mean bone in her body.

He shook his head. This was tough. Real tough. And not just on her, but on everyone in the family. He wondered how Patrick was doing. Jack couldn't imagine what it would be like to stand by and see the woman you loved go through something like this.

Still thinking about Jan and Patrick, he went back to his dinner preparations, but the enthusiasm he'd felt earlier had disappeared. He tried to put himself in Patrick's shoes. He knew one thing. If he was Patrick, he'd be madder than hell. Jan didn't deserve

this. What was she? Thirty-eight? Thirty-nine? And now, having to face cancer? And they had four kids. What if Jan didn't pull through? Weren't there enough crappy marriages out there without something like this happening to two people who had a good marriage?

Kevin had said Sheila was really upset. Jack wondered if he should call her and tell her to take tomorrow off. He thought about it for a while, then decided that wasn't a good idea. She'd think he was giving her special treatment, and she wouldn't want that. If she wanted the day off, she'd ask. Maybe it was better for her to be at work, anyway. Take her mind off Jan.

But Jack had better keep a sharp eye on her tomorrow, because when a person was worried, they didn't concentrate their full attention on the job, and that could be a recipe for disaster with someone as new to the work as Sheila. He sure didn't want her getting hurt or causing anyone else to get hurt.

With that issue settled in his mind, he finally put the chops on to broil.

Talking to Jana had been one of the hardest things Sheila had ever had to do. Jana was scared to death, because she was old enough to know the dangers and possibilities of complications from breast cancer. In trying to reassure her, Sheila had to overcome her own fears. After stressing the recovery rate when a malignancy was found early enough, which surely

this had been, she emphasized how much Jan needed her oldest daughter's support.

"You know, honey, it's been proved that thinking along positive lines is a great help in healing, not only for the person who's sick, but for all the people around her. That's what we need to do. Think positive, because your mother needs that help from all of us."

"But I'm so scared, Aunt Sheila."

"I know you are. But try not to let it show, okay? Not just for your mom's sake, but for your sisters. Especially the younger ones. Now come on. Let me see a smile, and then let's go out and join the others. All right?"

"All right."

They walked out to the kitchen, and within minutes Sheila's father arrived. And soon the others were home, too, and everyone made an effort to keep up a cheerful front. Still, the evening was a strain for Sheila. Behind Jan's smile and upbeat outlook, she saw the fear—the same fear Sheila was trying to banish. And she knew her parents and Patrick were just as afraid.

Please, God, she prayed. *Please take care of Jan.*

At nine, Sheila knew it was time to go. Her parents were already gone, and the girls had all headed off to their rooms to get ready for bed. Now Patrick and Jan needed time alone.

"I'll walk you to the door," Jan said.

At the door, they hugged tightly. "Are you sure you don't want me to go with you tomorrow?"

Sheila asked again, even though Jan had already said no once.

"Wait," Jan said, drawing back and looking into Sheila's eyes. "It means a lot to me that you want to be there, but we don't have any idea yet what's going to happen. If..." She swallowed, and for just an instant, the fear was there, naked and stark. But somehow she managed to conquer it, and her eyes cleared. "If I have to have surgery, I'm sure they won't do it tomorrow. And really, that's the day I'd like you to be there."

Sheila nodded over the lump in her throat. Jan was so damned brave! Giving Jan a wobbly smile, she hugged her again. "I love you," she whispered.

"I love you, too."

Then, afraid she might break down, Sheila opened the front door and left.

Sheila had expected that she and Kenny would be digging trenches again the next day, but Jack surprised her.

"You two are going to learn how to frame today."

"Really?" Sheila said.

"Hey, man, that's cool," Kenny said. "That means I can ditch this shovel, right?"

"For now," Jack answered with a grin. "If you screw up too much on the framing, I might put you back on trench detail, though."

Kenny rolled his eyes.

Sheila was suspicious of this sudden generosity,

but she was too grateful to get off the digging detail to question it.

For the next few hours, it took all of Sheila's concentration to remember Jack's instructions and follow his example as he demonstrated each step of the framing process.

It was harder than it looked, she quickly realized. She'd been under the mistaken impression that it couldn't be *that* difficult to nail two pieces of lumber together, but there was more precision involved than first appeared.

Jack explained that the first step in framing a house was to build a deck, or floor, on top of the foundation. This provided a level work platform, after which the wall frames could be easily laid out and put together. Then he proceeded to show them how to build the deck.

Sheila watched him carefully, doing exactly what she was told. Kenny, too, paid close attention. She could hardly believe it when Jack said it was time to knock off for lunch. The morning had sped by.

Kenny immediately took off, but Sheila—who had added a few more sore muscles due to all the bending she'd done today—was slower to move.

"You eating here today?" Jack asked as she started to walk toward her car.

Sheila's pulse quickened. Was he going to ask her to go to lunch? "No," she said regretfully, "I was just going to eat my sandwich in the car. I thought I'd drive over to the office and see if Dad has heard anything from Patrick. You know about Jan, don't

you?'' Her mother said Kevin was planning to call Jack.

Jack nodded gravely. ''Yeah, Kevin told me. But you don't have to give up your lunch break. Here.'' He unhooked his cell phone and handed it to her. ''You can call your dad if you want.''

This simple act of kindness touched Sheila deeply. But she was so used to having to be on her guard around Jack, and so conditioned to the wise-crack reply to cover up her real feelings, it was hard for her to switch gears. ''Thanks.'' She accepted the phone, suddenly tongue-tied.

Their gazes met. Held.

For just an instant she saw a flicker of something in his eyes, something that she could have sworn was desire. Seeing it gave her a burst of hope. Then that something was gone, and she wondered if she'd imagined it because she so wanted it to be there.

''I'll bring the phone back to you when I'm finished,'' she managed to say.

He smiled. ''Okay.''

As she walked toward her car, she knew he was watching her, and it made her self-conscious. She would have given anything to know what he was thinking. *Had* that look in his eyes been her imagination? Or, as she so desperately wanted to believe, was he finally beginning to see her as a desirable woman?

It had been so sweet of him to offer her the use of his phone. She'd always known he had a tender side, although it emerged only rarely, and until now,

seldom around her. But she'd heard Kevin talk about the way Jack had helped his brother Mike both during and after his divorce. And she knew Jack was awfully good to his mother, too.

Funny how she didn't view Jack's thoughtfulness with his cell phone as special treatment on the job the way she would have if he'd broken the company rule about the phone in the trailer. She quickly realized the reason. The cell phone was his personal property, and she was officially on her lunch hour.

Reaching her car, she forced her thoughts away from Jack. There'd be plenty of time to think about him again. Right now, Jan was the important one. Sheila got in the car and closed the door before punching in the numbers of her parents' house on Jack's cell phone.

''Mom?'' Sheila said when her mother picked up. ''Have you heard anything from Patrick yet?''

''He called about fifteen minutes ago.''

Sheila held her breath. ''And?''

''Jan's going to have surgery tomorrow morning.''

''A mastectomy?''

''No. From what Patrick said, they're just going to go in and remove the cancerous lump, some of the tissue around it and the lymph nodes. Then afterward, she'll have radiation.''

Sheila finally expelled her breath. ''What are her chances?'' She tried to keep the anxiety she felt out of her voice, because she knew how her mother worried.

''Patrick said the doctor was encouraging. He told them there was a good chance they could stop this thing from going any farther. I guess the percentages are favorable in cases like these.''

''Oh, God, I hope he's right.''

''He was cautious, though. He said Jan would have to have follow-up X rays every three months to make sure there were no other outbreaks.''

Sheila wanted to think positive as she'd advised Jana, but there was a knot of fear in her chest that she couldn't dispel. She made an effort to keep her voice upbeat, though. ''Did you talk to Jan at all?''

''No. She hadn't been moved into a room yet, and Patrick was using the pay phone in the hall.''

They talked a few minutes more, then hung up. When the connection was broken, Sheila sat unmoving. She stared out the car window, but she saw nothing. Jan would be okay. She would beat this thing. She had to. Anything else was unacceptable.

Jack took one look at Sheila's face and knew she was upset. He could see she was fighting tears, and he wanted, more than anything, to comfort her. Yet he was all too aware of their setting and how much talk and speculation such a display would fuel.

So he contented himself with shielding her from the curious eyes he knew were turned their way by standing between her and the work area.

''Bad news?''

''No. Not really. It's just...'' Her voice trailed off. ''It's just that this is so scary.''

"You okay?"

She nodded, but her beautiful gray eyes were clouded with anxiety. "Look, Jack, I know I just started this job, but I'm going to need to take tomorrow off. Jan's having her surgery then."

"Hey, no problem. Why don't you take the rest of today, too?"

She swallowed. "I can finish out the day."

"Sheila," he said more firmly. "Listen to me. You're upset. When people are upset, they're a danger to themselves and everybody else. Go home." He squeezed her arm.

She bowed her head. Seemed to be struggling with herself. Finally she nodded and looked up. The smile she gave him was a good try. "You're right. Thanks." Then she really *did* smile. "You're not going to hold this against me, are you?"

He smiled slowly. "No. Now get out of here before I change my mind."

After showering and changing into clean clothes, Sheila drove over to her parents' house.

"What are you doing here?" her mother said, obviously surprised to see her.

"Jack told me to go home. I guess he figured I was a hazard on the job."

Her mother smiled sadly. "That was nice of him."

"Yes, it was."

"I suppose you want to go to the hospital."

"I thought I would, unless you need me to stay and help with the girls."

"I can handle the girls. No, you go on to the hospital. Jan needs you a lot more than I do."

"Do you know how to get there?"

"Yes. Patrick called and gave me the directions. He wants us to bring the girls tonight."

Sheila wrote down the particulars, then kissed her mother goodbye and headed for Austin. She found the medical center, which was centrally located off I-35, without too much difficulty. By three o'clock—armed with magazines and a couple of books she thought Jan might like—Sheila was walking into Jan's room.

Patrick jumped up. "I'm going to go get a Coke or something and let you two girls talk for a while."

Jan's amused eyes met Sheila's. Once Patrick was gone, she said, "He was going nuts sitting here."

Sheila was amazed at how calm Jan seemed. Even cheerful. She said as much.

Jan smiled ruefully. "It's the strangest thing. I was scared to death yesterday, but now that I know what's wrong and how they'll treat it, I'm fine. It's hard to explain, but not knowing was so much worse."

"No, I think I understand. It's..." Sheila searched for what she wanted to say. "It's a matter of control. When you don't know, you feel out of control."

"Exactly," Jan said. "And you know, I have perfect confidence in Dr. Vogle. He's wonderful, Sheila. You would love him. He made me feel so

good when he talked to me. He explained *everything*.'' She smiled. ''He was so sweet. He said in my shoes he would want to know exactly what was going to happen and why. And, you know, now I just feel everything's going to be okay.''

Suddenly Sheila did, too.

For the rest of the afternoon, she and Jan visited and gossiped about all the things they never seemed to have time to discuss. The time flew by, and before they knew it, Sheila's parents had arrived with the girls, and then it was dinnertime and Jan's tray arrived.

By seven, the rest of the family had put in an appearance, and Jan's room was filled with people who loved her and were determined to take her mind off tomorrow's events. At nine, the bell signalling that it was time for visitors to leave sounded, and all but Patrick—who was spending the night—started gathering up belongings.

Sheila waited until almost everyone else had said goodbye before giving Jan a hug and kiss. Her surgery was scheduled for eight o'clock in the morning, but they'd been told she would be taken in the surgery waiting area by six-thirty, so Sheila said, ''I'll be here by six.''

''Okay,'' Jan said.

They hugged one more time, then Sheila, accompanied by Glenn, who'd waited for her, walked out together.

''Where'd you park?'' he asked.

''I was lucky. Found a place near the front door.''

They rode silently down on the elevator, then he walked her to her car.

"How're things going at work?" he asked as she unlocked the driver's side door.

"I'm doing okay. Of course, I ache all over."

Glenn grinned. "Yeah, I remember."

They talked a minute or two more, then he hugged her good-night and made sure she got into her car safely before heading on to his own truck.

The ride home was faster than the ride to the medical center, because traffic wasn't as heavy, so Sheila was pulling into her parking slot at her apartment building a little after ten.

Her steps were slow as she climbed to the second floor. The strain of the day had taken its toll. Her head was pounding, and she knew she probably wouldn't sleep.

Reaching the door of her apartment, she heard the phone ringing, and just managed to get the door unlocked and grab the phone before the answering machine kicked in.

"Hello," she said breathlessly.

"Sheila? It's Jack."

Her heart leapt. Jack! "Hi."

"I was just wondering how Jan was doing. I called you earlier but there wasn't any answer, so I figured you were at the hospital."

"Yes. I just got home." She licked her lips. "Jan's doing okay. She's scared, I'm sure, but she's handling it."

"Yeah, well, she's a trouper."

"Yes." Suddenly, all the submerged worry of the past two days combined with the thoughtfulness she heard in his voice caused her eyes to fill with tears. She couldn't say more. She was too afraid she would break down.

"Sheila?" he said softly after a few silent moments passed. "You okay?"

"Yes," she whispered. "I—I'm fine."

"Good. Listen, tell Jan I called, okay?"

"I will." She had herself under control now. "And thanks, Jack."

"No thanks needed."

For hours afterward, as she lay sleepless and wide-eyed, the memory of the phone call comforted Sheila, for she knew Jack could have called Kevin and gotten the same information.

But he hadn't.

He'd called *her*.

Didn't that prove that he had some kind of feeling for her?

As always, when her mind veered in this direction, she felt guilty. She should be thinking about Jan, not herself. But no matter how many times she told herself this, her wayward thoughts continued to drift back to the man who had occupied the number-one spot in her heart for so many years.

It was obvious that his attitude toward Sheila was changing. He was no longer treating her like some kid. Even though, a lot of the time, he still gave her that look of hidden amusement, he was beginning to treat her like an adult. Like a friend.

For so long, Sheila had felt the situation with Jack was hopeless, that he would never see her as a desirable woman. But the developments of the past week had given her hope.

She fell asleep with a smile on her face.

Chapter Six

Sheila had been trying, without much success, to read as she and Patrick and Rose sat in the surgery waiting area for news of Jan. Sighing, she stuffed her novel into her tote and glanced up at the wall clock.

Ten o'clock.

Jan's doctor had told Patrick the surgery would only take about an hour, but so far, they'd had no word. Sheila chewed on her lower lip. She hoped the fact that two hours had gone by didn't mean anything bad. She glanced at Patrick, and just as she did, he looked up. She could see the same worry she felt reflected in his eyes.

"We'll hear soon," she said, giving him an encouraging smile.

He nodded, but his eyes stayed clouded.

A few seconds later, the phone at the waiting-area reception desk rang. The volunteer answered, then called out, "Callahan. Callahan Family."

Patrick jumped up, followed by Sheila and her mother. The volunteer held out the receiver, mouthing, "It's your wife's surgeon."

Patrick took the phone. "Yes? Yes. Uh-huh." There was a long pause while Patrick listened. Finally, just as Sheila was beginning to get scared that something *had* gone wrong, a huge grin split his face, and he gave Sheila and Rose a thumbs-up. "O*kay*. Thank you, Dr. Vogle. Thank you."

On the way back to their seats, Patrick happily gave them a rundown on what Jan's surgeon had told him. "Dr. Vogle said everything looks good. They removed the diseased tissue and the lymph nodes and enough surrounding tissue so that he feels, with radiation, Jan has a good chance for complete recovery."

The fears of the past few days lifted, and suddenly Sheila was aware of just how pervasive they'd been. "Oh, Patrick, that's great!"

"Thank you, Lord," Rose said fervently.

Sheila felt like dancing, she was so happy.

"Jan's on her way to recovery right now," Patrick said. "The doctor said they'll call us when she's awake and we can go back and see her."

An hour later, the call came, and they hurried to the recovery area. Jan, pale and groggy, gave them a weak smile when they entered. Sheila and her

mother stayed only a few minutes, figuring Patrick would want to be alone with Jan.

"We'll see you later," Sheila said, giving Jan's hand a squeeze.

Back in the waiting area, Sheila and Rose headed for the bank of pay phones.

"I'll call your father," Rose said. "I know he's waiting to hear. And I'll call Jan's brother." Jan's only sibling was in the army and stationed in Germany. As she spoke, Sheila's mother pulled out her telephone calling card.

"Okay. I'll call the guys." Sheila had the numbers of all her brothers' cell phones. She reached Glenn first, then Rory, then Kevin.

"You gonna call Jack?" Kevin asked as they were ending the call.

"Jack?"

"Yeah. He's worried, too."

"I...well, sure. I'll call him."

"You got his cell phone number?"

"No."

Kevin started to give her the number.

"Hold on a minute." Sheila rummaged in her purse for a pen and something to write on. She found an old business card and turned it over. "Okay."

Sheila would never have thought to call Jack, but now that Kevin had suggested it, she realized it was the thoughtful thing to do, especially after his evidenced concern the day before. As she punched in the numbers, her heart gave a little zing of antici-

pation. The number rang, and he answered almost immediately.

"Sheila? Is everything okay?"

She smiled. "Yes. Everything's terrific." She quickly explained what she'd been told.

"That's great. Tell Patrick and Jan I'm thinkin' about 'em, okay?"

"I will."

"Does Jan have a room number yet?"

"No, not yet. She's still in recovery."

"I wanted to send her some flowers. Do you think she'd like roses?"

"I'm sure she'd love roses, but don't send them here. The doctor told Patrick she would probably only be in overnight."

"Overnight?" Jack sounded incredulous.

"I know, it does seem awfully fast, but that's the way they do things nowadays."

"So she'll go home tomorrow?" He still sounded disbelieving.

"Unless there are problems, but we're thinking positive."

"All right. I'll wait and send 'em to the house, I guess."

"Good. Listen, Mom and I are tying up both the phones here, so I'd better go. I, um, I'll see you tomorrow."

He chuckled. "We haven't scared you off yet, huh?"

She smiled. "Nope."

"What if I put you back on the digging detail?"

"Even then."

"Okay, tiger, see you tomorrow."

Sheila was still grinning when she rejoined her mother, who had finished her last phone call and was once again sitting down.

Rose smiled. "Everybody was happy, huh?"

"Oh, yes. Everybody was happy."

But Sheila wasn't thinking about everybody. She was thinking about Jack. She was thinking how just the sound of his voice was enough to lift her spirits. She was also thinking how, now that Jan was truly on the road to recovery, there was no longer anything or anyone to distract her from her twin goals: proving to one and all that she had what it took to succeed at her job and proving to Jack that she was the woman for him.

Jack smiled as he turned off the phone. He still wasn't convinced Sheila belonged out here, but he had to hand it to her. She was determined. And if that determination spelled the difference between succeeding at the job or failing, Sheila would succeed. Unfortunately, determination alone wasn't enough. Like it or not, Sheila was operating under several handicaps. All you had to do was watch her work to see she wasn't as strong as the men. No matter how hard she tried, that fact alone could be hazardous, not just to her, but to the other guys. So as long as she was working for him, Jack would still have to keep a close eye on her.

"When's Sheila coming back?"

Jack blinked. He'd been so lost in his thoughts he hadn't seen Rick Clemmons, one of the oldest hands on his crew. "Tomorrow. Why?"

Rick, a beefy former fullback, grinned. "She improves the view around here, that's why. She's got a nice butt." When two of the other guys within hearing distance echoed their agreement, his grin expanded, especially when one of the guys made a crude gesture.

Jack saw red. "Listen, hotshot," he said through gritted teeth, turning his furious gaze from Rick to the other two and back again. "I told you guys before. She's Old Man Callahan's daughter. That means you'd better keep your eyes and your thoughts to your*self,* you hear?"

Rick held up his hands. "Jeez, man, cool it. I didn't mean nuthin'."

"Yeah, me neither," said the one who'd made the gesture. His expression said he thought Jack was nuts.

"Fine," Jack answered tightly. "Just remember you get paid to do a job, Clemmons. Not to ogle women." He glared at the other two, who had turned back to the job at hand and were acting as if they weren't listening. "That goes for all of you. Understand?"

As he strode away, he knew they were exchanging looks, probably wondering what his problem was, because in the past, Jack had made his share of coarse remarks right along with them. But hell, he'd never meant anything by them. And he'd sure

as hell never said anything about any woman specifically, let alone a woman like Sheila.

It made him mad all over again to think of those lowlifes talking about Sheila's body the way they had. And yet, could he really blame them? Sheila was a beautiful woman with a great body. And they were just guys, not saints.

He kicked at a soda can someone had carelessly tossed on the ground. *I don't need this. I do not need this.*

Unfortunately for him, he was stuck with the problem. And somehow, he would have to deal with it.

Sheila went to work the following morning revved up and raring to go. Last night, she had decided on a plan of attack regarding Jack, and today she was going to put it into motion. One thing Sheila knew for sure: nothing made a man sit up and take notice of a woman more than the interest of someone else. And since Kenny had *already* hinted that he liked her, she figured playing up to Kenny was the way to go. He was cute, so it would be no hardship to flirt with him, but the big advantage with Kenny was the fact that Jack could hardly help but notice if Sheila paid extra attention to him.

She and Kenny were on the framing detail again, and as he had from the beginning, Jack kept a close eye on them, especially her. Sheila wished she could believe his interest was in her as a woman, but she was afraid he was just nervous about her ability to

do the job without screwing up. Well, she hated to disappoint him, but she had no intention of screwing up.

"Man, he's watchin' us like a hawk," Kenny complained about midmorning. "He makes me nervous."

"You don't have any reason to worry. It's *me* he doesn't trust," Sheila grumbled.

Kenny grinned. "Nah, I think he just likes lookin' at *you.*"

Sheila almost said, *Do you really think so?* but stopped herself in time. It wouldn't do for Kenny to suspect how she felt about Jack. It wouldn't do for *any* of the guys to suspect her true feelings. Oh, man, she could just imagine what they'd have to say if they did. They would tease her unmercifully. Worse, they would let Jack know, and then her situation would be untenable. So she said, "I doubt that," and turned away so Kenny wouldn't pursue the subject.

Still, all morning she felt Jack's eyes on her, and his scrutiny made her nervous. A couple of times she almost hit her finger when she was driving in a nail. The last time it happened, he saw it.

"A construction site is a dangerous place," he said, walking up to her. "If you don't pay close attention, you can get hurt."

Sheila looked up, meeting his shadowed gaze. "I *was* paying attention."

"Didn't look that way to me."

Sheila had to bite back another remark, knowing

arguing with him wouldn't do any good. He stood there a while longer, watching as she resumed her work. Gritting her teeth, she was doubly careful to do everything exactly right, and after a few moments, he walked away.

But he didn't go far. And he didn't stop watching her. About eleven-thirty, she had just finished nailing the last piece of lumber in her assigned section and sat back on her haunches to view her work when, out of the corner of her eye, she saw Jack approaching again. She turned to see what he wanted this time, and their eyes met.

The events of the next few seconds unfolded like a slow-motion movie. Jack, still looking at her, stepped on a stray piece of lumber, which flipped up. His arms flailed, he lost his balance, and the next thing she knew, he was flat on his back.

All work stopped, and six pairs of eyes—all Jack's crew who were in the immediate vicinity—watched as Jack hurriedly got to his feet. His face was red, and Sheila knew he was embarrassed. What had happened to him was something that only happened to rank amateurs, never to seasoned pros.

A couple of the guys were smiling, and one of them—a guy named Tony who was a real practical joker—said, "Hey, Jack, best you keep *your* mind on *your* work." A couple of the others snickered. Rick Clemmons laughed out loud, and Tony grinned, proud of himself.

"Yeah," somebody else said, "if you don't pay close attention, you can get hurt."

''Uh-oh,'' Kenny muttered beside her.

Sheila looked at Jack. His face was set in grim lines. ''Who left that piece of lumber lying there?'' he said.

Nobody said a word. Long minutes passed. Then somebody snorted. Jack's head whipped around, and he glared at the men, who were still standing there watching. ''Show's over,'' he ground out. ''Get back to work.''

They did, but not without muffled laughter and sidelong looks at Jack, who stalked off.

Sheila felt kind of bad that Jack had had to bear the brunt of the guys' jokes, but it really served him right. If he hadn't been so all-fired sure she was going to screw up, he would have been paying attention to where he was walking. Besides, it was kind of satisfying to see the cocky Jack Kinsella taken down a peg or two.

''Oh, boy,'' Kenny said.

Sheila tried not to smile, but she lost the battle.

''You know, even though that was funny, I kinda feel sorry for him, 'cause no guy wants to look stupid in front of the men who work for him.'' Kenny grinned and lowered his voice. ''Especially when one of the men is a woman.''

Sheila nodded. She hoped this little episode didn't mean Jack would be even harder on her in the future. No sense worrying about it, though, because there wasn't much she could do about it if he was. Sighing, she looked at her watch. It was lunchtime. ''Let's go eat.''

Kenny, always agreeable, said, ‘‘Okay.’’

They crossed the street and walked to where they’d parked their vehicles. Sheila unlocked her car and took her lunch and a bottle of water out of her cooler. Then she joined Kenny, who was already sitting on his tailgate drinking a Dr. Pepper and eating a ham sandwich and chips. As usual, country music blasted from one of the trucks. A Randy Travis song if Sheila wasn’t mistaken.

Sheila unwrapped her chicken salad sandwich and took a bite. For a few minutes, they sat and ate in companionable silence. The Randy Travis song finished, and a Shania Twain song followed. Sheila hummed along.

‘‘Looks like it might rain,’’ Kenny said.

‘‘They’ve been predicting rain for days.’’

‘‘What’ll happen if it does? Do you know?’’

‘‘You mean out here?’’

‘‘Yeah.’’

‘‘They’ll send us home.’’

‘‘With pay?’’ Kenny said hopefully.

Sheila grimaced. ‘‘No, unfortunately, not with pay. We only get paid the hours we work.’’

‘‘That’s a bummer.’’

‘‘I know. My dad feels bad about that, but he’d go under if he had to pay for all the bad-weather days. That’s one of the reasons we get such a good hourly rate when we *are* working.’’

Kenny thought about that for a while, then said, ‘‘So, Sheila, what do you do for fun?’’ He balled

up the plastic wrap from his sandwich and tossed it into a nearby trash can.

"Oh, I don't know. Lots of things."

"Ever go dancin'?"

"I like to, but there's no place to dance in Rainbow's End. Unless..." She made a face. "You want to go join the old fogies at the Knights of Columbus Hall."

Kenny laughed. "Somehow I can't see you there."

"No. Me, either."

"I did hear they're gonna start having a band now on Friday and Saturday nights at Pot O' Gold."

"You're kidding. Since when?"

"Since last week. They took out the two pool tables in the back to make room for a dance floor and even put in a small stage for the band."

"I can't believe it. Boy, I'll bet my brothers won't like this development."

"Why not?"

She rolled her eyes. "Because they think of Pot O' Gold as *their* pub. You know, a guy kind of place. Pool, dartboards, sports on the big screen TV."

"But there are always girls there."

"I know. But the girls only come because the guys are there, not because they really like the place. Wonder why Big Jim decided to make the change?" Big Jim Sullivan, so called because he topped three hundred pounds, was the longtime owner of the pub.

"I hear his son pushed for it. He said they could

double their business if they added the dancing. I mean, let's face it. Pool doesn't bring anybody in who wouldn't be there, anyway.''

''I'm sure Joe's right. It's just so hard to believe. I didn't think Pot O' Gold would ever change.''

''Hey, it's called progress.'' He grinned and added, ''So whadda ya think?''

''What do I think about what?''

''Want to go there tonight? Check it out?''

''You mean, you and me?''

Kenny's dark eyes twinkled. ''Yeah. You and me.'' He drained his drink.

Sheila could see Jack in the distance. He was standing talking to one of the guys, and the sun glinted off the top of his hard hat. The hard hat that covered his hard head. The same hard head that always spent its Friday nights at Pot O' Gold. She smiled slowly, turning to look at Kenny. ''I think that's a great idea.''

''So tell me all about this Kenny,'' Carrie said. She was sitting cross-legged on Sheila's bed as she watched Sheila get dressed.

''He's cute.'' Sheila held up two dresses—one red, one black. ''Which one should I wear? Or do you think they're both too dressy?''

''The red one,'' Carrie said. ''Cute, huh? How cute?''

''Real cute.''

''Is he tall?''

Sheila rolled her eyes. ''What is it with you and tall men?''

Carrie took a bite of the Granny Smith apple she'd found in Sheila's crisper. ''I like 'em tall. I make no apologies for that.''

''He's tall enough. Maybe five-ten.''

''What color is his hair?''

''Carrie, you're going to see him.''

''I know, but tell me anyway.''

Sheila sighed. ''He's got black hair. Thick black hair and dark eyes. He looks kind of like that cop who used to be on *Law and Order*. You know the one I mean?''

''That Benjamin whatshisname?''

Sheila nodded.

Carrie whistled. ''Oooo, he's more than cute. He's *hot*. So what time is this Hot Kenny picking you up?''

''Carrie!''

''Oh, okay, I'll be good.''

Sheila grinned. ''He's picking me up at eight.''

''I better be goin' then, huh?''

''It's only seven. You don't have to leave yet.''

''Well, I want to go home and take a shower and get to the pub myself.''

''All right. I'll see you later, then.''

Carrie left and Sheila finished getting ready. She almost didn't follow Carrie's advice about the red dress, but after looking at the much tighter and shorter skirt on the black dress, she decided Carrie

was right. The red dress would be easier to dance in.

At eight, she was ready, and Kenny—looking great in black slacks and open-necked black shirt—arrived a few minutes later.

"Hey, look at you," he said, giving her an appreciative once-over. "Nice dress."

Sheila grinned. "Thanks. I clean up good."

"You can say that again."

"I clean up good."

He laughed. "I think we're gonna have fun tonight."

Sheila thought about Jack. She thought about Jack seeing her with Kenny. "You know what, Kenny? I think you're right."

Because the pub was crowded, Jack paid for a beer at the bar, then headed for his usual table at Pot O' Gold. He said a few hellos to the regulars, then settled in to wait for Kevin to show up. He was glad the day was nearly over. Every time he thought about the way he'd fallen earlier, he cringed. Bad enough he'd been so focused on Sheila and what she was doing that he'd had the fall in the first place, but to do it in front of the guys—man, that was bad.

He'd been right to begin with. The construction site was no place for a woman, especially a woman like Sheila.

Well, no more Mr. Nice Guy. Today had shown him that lately he'd been going soft in the head. From now on, he wasn't cutting her one inch of

slack, and if she couldn't take it, well, tough. Let her quit. In fact, he *wanted* her to quit. Having her on his crew was a terrible idea. The king of terrible ideas. In fact, having Sheila Callahan anywhere in his vicinity was a disaster in the making.

Jack wondered how long it would take him to live down today's episode. He had a feeling he hadn't heard the last of it. Well, he'd just have to grin and bear it. Pretend the guys weren't getting to him when they ribbed him about it. Because if he knew anything about construction workers, he knew this: the minute you let them see you had any kind of weakness, they'd pounce on it and never let up. A construction site was like a jungle in that only the strong survived.

''Hey, Jack, I hear you had a little accident today.''

Jack looked up to see Kevin grinning down at him. ''Bad news travels fast,'' he said mildly. He took a slug of his beer, determined not to let Kevin or anyone else think he minded.

Kevin sat down. He was still grinning. ''Rumor has it you were so busy watching Sheila you weren't looking where you were going.''

''Yeah, well, Rumor's got a big mouth.''

Kevin laughed. ''I'm sorry. It's just that I'm so damned glad *I'm* not havin' to be her baby-sitter.'' Kevin looked at Jack's beer. ''I need one of those.'' He waved at Kitty O'Brien, one of the two waitresses Big Jim employed.

''Be there in a minute,'' she called.

Jack watched Kitty deftly serve the next table. She was a good-looking woman, but he'd never been interested. There was an old saying about not doing your business in your own backyard, and Kitty definitely fell into that category.

Jack liked hanging out at Pot O' Gold, but his comfort level would be ruined if Kitty had a problem with him. And in his experience, when a love affair went south, the lady in question *always* had a problem with him.

Nope, like Sheila, Kitty was out-of-bounds. Still, he thought with lazy amusement, it was fun to flirt with her.

She turned around just then and caught him watching her. Her eyes twinkled as she walked toward their table. ''Well, hello-o-o, Jack,'' she said, drawing out the last syllable in her greeting and giving it a seductive lilt. ''I didn't see you come in.'' She stood closer to him than she needed to, making sure he had a good view of her generous bosom. ''What can I get you two?''

Kevin grinned. ''I need a beer. And my friend here needs another.''

She gave Jack a mock frown. ''Where'd you get that beer? Is someone else getting my tips?''

He laughed. ''I knew you'd be busy tonight with this crowd, so I got it myself.''

''What a thoughtful man you are.'' Her eyes met Kevin's. ''Isn't Jack a thoughtful man?''

Kevin made a face. ''I can think of a lot of things Jack has been called, but that wasn't one of them.''

After a few more minutes of meaningless banter, she said, "Two beers coming right up." She walked away, hips swaying.

"That is one sexy woman," Kevin said. It was his standard remark each time they saw Kitty.

Jack shrugged. "Yep. That she is."

"So why haven't you ever asked her out?"

"Why haven't *you?*"

"She's not interested in *me.*"

"She's not interested in me, either."

Kevin gave him a knowing look. "C'mon, Jack. You know she is."

Jack opened his mouth to answer when, out of the corner of his eye, something caught his attention. He turned, and the answer froze on his lips. It was a moment before his brain registered what his eyes were seeing.

Sheila.

Sheila, dressed in a clingy red dress.

Sheila, laughing up at...*Kenny Romero!*

Some part of Jack's brain knew he was staring, but he seemed incapable of looking away. And as he looked, an unfamiliar emotion gripped him. An emotion he hadn't felt since he was a freshman in high school with a crush on the most popular girl in the sophomore class. An emotion he had never expected to feel again.

Jack Kinsella, champion breaker of female hearts, was jealous.

Chapter Seven

Sheila waved in the general direction of her brother and Jack.

''I hope you don't want to sit with them,'' Kenny said into her ear.

''Of course not.'' But Sheila would have *loved* to sit with them. That way, she could have been sure Jack would notice her all evening long the way he was noticing her now. ''I just thought we'd say hello.'' Because Jack was still watching their approach, she gave Kenny her most brilliant smile. In answer, he squeezed her waist.

''Hey,'' Kevin said. ''Look who's here.'' He stood, and he and Kenny shook hands as Sheila introduced them.

''Hello, Jack,'' she said, finally turning her gaze his way.

"Hello, Sheila. Kenny."

Did his smile seem forced? Or was that simply wishful thinking on her part?

"You two want to sit with us?" Kevin asked, indicating the two empty chairs at their table.

Kenny shook his head. "Thanks, but I see a table over there closer to the dance floor. We came for the dancing, didn't we, Sheila?"

This time her smile was flirty. "Yes, we did."

"When's the band start, anyway?" Kenny said to Kevin.

"Nine o'clock, I think."

"Worst idea I ever heard of," Jack said. "Dancing'll ruin this place."

"Oh, do you think so?" Sheila said. "Personally, I think it's great. But then, I'm counting on Kenny not having two left feet like you guys."

Kenny grinned and put his arm around her waist again. "I'm sure you'll inspire me."

Sheila darted a glance at Jack and was gratified to see him glowering. Of course, his bad mood might have nothing to do with her, but she preferred to think otherwise.

"Here comes the band now," Kevin said.

Sheila turned around and saw several guys carrying instrument cases wending their way through the crowd.

"We'd better go grab that table," Kenny said, "before someone else gets it."

Sheila gave a jaunty little wave, but Jack was no longer looking. She refused to be disheartened,

though. The evening was young. And they hadn't started dancing yet. When they did, she'd make very sure he saw her.

Kenny snagged the table in question only seconds before another couple tried to claim it. Sheila maneuvered so that she was seated facing Jack's table. He wasn't looking in her direction, but she felt sure as soon as the music started, he would be.

She looked around. The place was practically full already and it was still early. The dancing had definitely made a difference. Just then, she spied Carrie coming in with Lisa Fulton, another friend from high school days. Sheila waved.

A few moments later, Carrie spotted her. After Carrie said something to Lisa, the two headed in their direction.

''Hi,'' Carrie said. Although she was speaking to Sheila, her eyes were on Kenny.

Sheila smiled in amusement. ''Kenny, I'd like you to meet two friends of mine. Carrie Ferguson and Lisa Fulton.''

They chatted for a couple of minutes, and from the approving look on Carrie's face, Sheila knew Kenny was a hit. Then Carrie and Lisa left them to go and join some other friends.

''I see the waitress coming,'' Kenny said after they were gone. ''What do you want to drink?''

''I'll just have a diet soda.''

''That's it?''

''Uh-huh.'' Sheila didn't drink much. Wine made

her sleepy, and she didn't like the taste of beer. Besides, tonight she wanted all her wits about her.

A few seconds later, Kitty O'Brien reached their table. Sheila had always liked Kitty, who, at thirty-four, was the same age as Sheila's brother Keith. She knew, from the grapevine, that Kitty's marriage had been disastrous. It was common knowledge that Doug Paglia had knocked her around. Sheila had always thought it would take only once for her to walk out on a guy like that, but then again, she'd never been in that position. Maybe women whose husbands or boyfriends beat them kept hoping things would change, and that was why they stuck it out, only leaving when they finally realized the situation was hopeless.

''Hi, Sheila!'' Kitty said. ''It's good to see you. You haven't been here for a while.''

Sheila smiled warmly. ''I know. Kitty, this is Kenny Romero. He's new in town.''

''Really? And you moved here on purpose?''

Kenny laughed. ''Yeah, I did.''

''Where are you from?''

''I grew up in San Angelo. But my dad retired and he and my mother moved here a couple of years ago. Then I got laid off, and they kept tellin' me how nice Rainbow's End was, so I decided to check it out for myself.''

''Rainbow's End is great if you like boring, boring and more boring,'' Kitty said with a rueful smile.

''You live here,'' Kenny pointed out.

"Kitty takes care of her father," Sheila interjected.

Kitty nodded. "If it wasn't for Dad, I'd be outta here so-o-o-o fast."

Kenny's gaze moved to Sheila. "I don't know. I think *I'm* goin' to like it here a lot."

"Well, we're always glad for another paying customer," Kitty said. "And on that note, what can I get you?"

Kenny gave her their drink orders, and after a few more minutes of chatter, she left. By then, the band had started tuning up. A few minutes later, they launched into a fast number Sheila didn't recognize, although it had a toe-tapping rhythm that made her feet itch.

"Want to try it?" Kenny said.

"Sure."

Sheila loved to dance. Her mother had seen to it that both she and her brothers learned at an early age, and Sheila had taken to dancing like a duck to water.

Kenny turned out to be a terrific dancer. He wasn't a show-off, like some guys Sheila had seen or danced with. He just had a great sense of rhythm and was a masterful lead. Most importantly, he knew how to make his partner look good. She was thrilled with Kenny's skill—not just because it would make her evening much more enjoyable—but because she knew people would be watching them.

And that included Jack.

The band was good, too. In addition to the fast

number, the first set included a slow tune, a country two-step and then a terrific song with a Latin beat. The Latin number was fast and allowed Sheila and Kenny to really let loose.

"Wow!" he said at the end when he'd twirled her in a fast triple spin that ended in his arms. "You're good!"

She laughed. "You're *wonderful.*" Exhilarated, she sneaked a peek in Jack's direction. But her elation was short-lived, because Jack wasn't looking at them. In fact, he was talking to Kitty O'Brien, and as Sheila watched, he reached up and pulled Kitty down onto his lap. Kitty was laughing and making no attempt to pull away.

Pain sliced through Sheila. She didn't want to watch, but she couldn't seem to help herself. It was only when she saw Jack nuzzle Kitty's neck that she tore her eyes away from the hurtful scene.

Tears stung her eyelids and, furious with herself, she forced them back. *I hate him. I hate him.* But no matter how many times she told herself this, she knew it wasn't true. If she really hated him, she wouldn't care how many women he flirted with or made love to. *Oh, God, I wish I did hate him. Everything would be so much easier.*

For the rest of the evening, she tried not to think about Jack. She and Kenny danced every set, and while she was on the floor, she actually managed to forget about him and enjoy herself. But the moment the set ended, her eyes inevitably sought him out. As far as she could tell, Jack was paying no attention

to her at all. She might as well not have existed. Instead, he was either laughing and talking with her brothers—Rory and Glenn had now joined him and Kevin—or flirting with Kitty or some other unattached woman. He was also drinking a lot, if Sheila was any judge, for he always seemed to have a fresh beer.

She was completely disheartened. Her plan had failed. Jack couldn't care less who she was with or what she was doing. She was also ashamed of herself, because Kenny was really a nice guy who didn't deserve to be used the way she'd tried to use him tonight. So shortly before midnight, she turned to him and said, "Would you mind if we called it a night? It's been a really stressful week, and I think it's catching up with me. I'm suddenly feeling exhausted."

"Hey," he said, "no problem. You want to go now?"

She nodded.

He kept his hand firmly around her waist as they walked out. They didn't stop at her brothers' table, and Sheila was glad. She knew they would tease her, and she wasn't in the mood for it. Besides, she had no desire to put on a false face for Jack's benefit.

As Kenny drove her home, Sheila thought about what she would do when they got to the apartment. She hoped Kenny didn't try to kiss her, but she was afraid he would. It wouldn't be a hardship to kiss him back, but she knew it would be wrong. Better

to be honest with him and nip this thing before it went any further.

Sure enough, when they got to her place, he insisted on walking her to the door, and she knew from the expression in his eyes that he wanted to kiss her.

"I had a great time tonight," he said softly, leaning closer.

"I did, too. Thanks for asking me."

He smiled down at her. "I want to do it again, real soon."

As gently as she could, Sheila said, "I don't think that's a good idea, Kenny."

He frowned and drew back slightly.

She laid her hand on his forearm. "I'm sorry. When you asked me out, I thought it might work, but the truth is, I'm in love with someone else, and it…it's not fair to use you as a substitute just because he doesn't want me."

For a moment, Kenny didn't say anything. Then he sighed. "I'm sorry, too, Sheila. I think you're terrific. All I can say is, whoever the guy is, he must be crazy. Or blind."

"He's neither," Sheila said. "Just not interested."

Kenny touched her cheek. "You know, maybe I don't mind being used. Maybe if you go out with me a few times, you'll forget about this other guy. Shoot, I'm willing to take a chance, 'cause I think you're worth it."

Sheila smiled sadly. "That's the nicest thing any-

one's said to me in a long time, and I'll never forget it, Kenny. But it's hopeless, I'm afraid."

"Oh, well. Can't blame a guy for trying." Then he leaned over and kissed her cheek. "If you change your mind, you know where to find me."

Jack knew he was going to have a granddaddy of a hangover tomorrow, but right then he didn't care. All night, he'd been in a frenzy of frustration. Dammit, anyway. What could Sheila have been thinking flaunting herself like that? Didn't she know she was just asking for trouble? It was bad enough she'd worn that clinging dress that left nothing to the imagination, but then she'd made matters ten times worse by the way she'd been dancing.

The image of her and Kenny on the dance floor was permanently burned into Jack's brain. As far as Jack was concerned, their dancing had been a blatant sexual exhibition. Hell, all a person had had to do was look at them for a while to know exactly what was going through Kenny's mind, at least, and exactly where the two of them would end up the evening.

Jack couldn't understand why her brothers seemed so unconcerned. After Sheila and Kenny left, he'd suggested to Kevin that maybe he should have a talk with Sheila.

"Hey, she's twenty-five years old," Kevin said. "I'm not gonna tell her what to do. It wouldn't do any good, anyway. Sheila has a mind of her own. Besides, I like Kenny. He seems like a nice guy."

Jack had liked Kenny, too, but that was before he'd realized what an opportunist he was. ''Guys like Kenny want one thing and one thing only,'' he grumbled.

''You're being ridiculous, Jack,'' Kevin said. ''I mean, let's face it. All guys want one thing in the beginning. I'm sure Sheila knows that.''

''From what I could see,'' Glenn interjected, ''I think he really likes her. Anyway, Sheila can take care of herself.''

''Likes her? Is that what you call it? He was slobbering all over her! Sheila is your sister, for crying out loud. I'd think you'd want to look out for her best interests.'' Furious with them and their obtuseness, Jack took another slug of his beer.

Rory gave him a thoughtful look. ''If I didn't know better, I'd say you were jealous, Jack.''

Jack slammed his bottle down. ''Jealous! There isn't a woman alive that could make me jealous.'' He glared at Rory. ''Hell, I'm just concerned about *your* sister, which you're obviously not. Fine. Don't pay any attention to me. But just remember this. When Sheila gets into trouble, you'll only have yourselves to blame, 'cause I warned you.'' So saying, he stood up and whistled for Kitty. Motioning that he needed another beer, he avoided the eyes of Sheila's brothers and silently fumed.

Later that night, at home in his apartment, no matter how he tried, Jack could not rid himself of the picture of Kenny and Sheila together. He kept re-

membering Kenny's possessive hand at her waist as they'd walked out of the pub. The way he'd looked at her. The way she'd looked at him.

He imagined them arriving at Sheila's apartment. Kissing. Touching. He saw them going inside. Standing in the dark. Kissing some more. He saw Kenny unzipping Sheila's dress. Exposing that creamy skin. The dress falling in a silky heap around her ankles.

He groaned as he imagined Sheila standing there in some filmy kind of underwear that barely covered that delectable body. Kenny's hands would tremble as he unhooked her bra. Touched her breasts. Put his mouth to those perfect little peaks.

Jack gritted his teeth. The pictures were driving him crazy, but no matter what he did, he couldn't get rid of them. Even after he fell asleep, he dreamed of Sheila and Kenny.

The next morning wasn't any better. It certainly didn't help that the hangover he'd anticipated was even worse than he'd imagined it would be: a relentless pounding that felt as if two giant hands were pummeling his head. After two strong cups of coffee, he put on his workout clothes and headed for the park, where he spent the next hour trying to sweat out the poison in his body and the images in his brain.

The workout made him feel fractionally better, and after a long, hot shower, he almost felt human again. Ready now for food, he fixed himself a scrambled egg sandwich, which he downed with

half a carton of juice. When he was finished he thought about the rest of the day and what he wanted to do with it. He knew what he didn't want to do: sit here with nothing to occupy his mind but things he'd rather forget.

Hitting on the perfect solution, he picked up the phone and called his mother.

"How'd you like some company this weekend?"

"Jack! Of course. I'd love to see you."

"You sure? I don't want to interfere if you have plans."

"The only plans I had were getting my laundry done. Otherwise, I'm free. When are you coming?"

"I was planning to leave now." He looked at his watch. It was nearly noon. "I should be there by four." His mother had moved to Houston shortly after she and his father divorced. She now worked as a secretary for one of the big oil companies and had recently bought herself a town house that she'd been dying to show off.

"Great. I'll be here."

Jack spent the three-plus-hour drive listening to CDs and purposely keeping his mind as far away from Sheila as he could get it. He tapped his fingers against the steering wheel in time to the music of Asleep at the Wheel doing old Bob Wills standards, sang along with Patsy Cline, then let all his concerns soar away with a soundtrack from the Paris concert of the Three Tenors.

Fifteen minutes before four, he pulled into the driveway of his mother's town home on the north-

west side of the city. Before he'd lifted his duffel bag out, she was walking out the door.

At fifty-six, dressed in jeans and a dark green sweater, Dorothy Kinsella looked ten years younger. Trim and petite, she had green eyes that sparkled with enthusiasm and a zest for life she had rediscovered since the split with his father. Her hair, still dark—although Jack suspected the color was helped along by her hairdresser—was cut short and curled softly around her face.

They hugged, then his mother stood back to look at him. "Still as handsome as ever," she pronounced.

Jack grinned. "And just as ornery."

She laughed. "That's a given." Wryly, she added, "After all, some of your genes came from your father."

Now it was Jack's turn to laugh.

"Speaking of," his mother said, "how's he doing?"

"Fine, I guess. I don't talk to him much." After the divorce Jack's father had moved to Arkansas where he could indulge his passion for fishing year-round.

Dorothy nodded. "I'm sure he's very happy."

It was funny, but she seemed more interested in Jack's father now than she ever had before. Just proved what Jack had always believed: that marriage—instead of strengthening and improving a relationship—more often ruined it.

"Well, come on in."

Proudly, she led him from room to room. The town home was two stories tall, with an L-shaped living/dining room combination, guest bath, laundry room and kitchen on the first floor, and two bedrooms with two full bathrooms on the second floor. In the back on ground level was a covered patio where his mother indulged her passion for flowers and plants. On the second level, a balcony opened up off the master bedroom. The only amenity the town home didn't have was a garage, although his mother explained that the two covered parking slots outside her back gate belonged to her. ''You can move your truck around and park it next to my car,'' she said.

After she'd given him a complete tour, she said, ''Well, what do you think of it? Isn't it nice?''

''It's perfect.''

''I think so.'' She sighed happily. ''You know, I never realized how much I would love living alone. It's wonderful.''

''You don't have to tell me. I've always liked living alone.''

Her face sobered. She studied him thoughtfully for a moment. ''You know, Jack, it's different for me. Your father and I married young. I was only eighteen. I'd never lived alone. I went straight from my parents' home to our shared home, and a year later, I was a mother. I never really had a chance to taste freedom or sow any oats before I had to grow up and face reality. So, of course, I'm enjoying this independence now.

"But you *have* been free, and for a long time. I have to be honest with you. I'd be very sad if you never found anyone to share your life with, because even though your dad's and my marriage didn't work out, I still believe in marriage. And I don't regret mine. Not for a second. After all, it gave me you and Mike. And it's given me two wonderful grandchildren. I don't want you to miss out on that."

Jack didn't know what to say. He'd had no idea she felt this way. In fact, he'd bragged to Kevin more than a few times about how his mother never put pressure on him to marry the way Rose Callahan did to her sons.

Dorothy grimaced. "You're thinking I should mind my own business, aren't you?"

Putting his arm around her shoulder, Jack said, "No, I was just surprised. You've never said anything like this before."

"I never wanted to be one of those pushy mothers," she admitted. "But lately, I don't know, I've felt kind of bad about you. Maybe if your father and I had had a better marriage you wouldn't be so—"

"Listen," he said, interrupting. "It's not your fault I feel the way I do about marriage. It's just not for me, that's all."

She nodded, but she didn't seem convinced.

"Thing is, I've never met anyone I could even imagine spending the rest of my life with." But even as he said the words, Sheila's face floated through

his mind. Disturbed by the association, he pushed the image away.

His mother's sober expression disappeared as she suddenly chuckled. "It's probably all to the good you feel the way you do, because I'd actually pity the poor woman who had to put up with you."

"Well, thanks a lot," Jack said with mock indignation. "I'm not *that* bad."

"You're a stubborn mule, and you know it."

After that, they moved on to a discussion about Mike, then talked about Dorothy's job, and ended with her telling him about a cousin of his who had just been diagnosed with cancer.

"It's such a shame," she said. "Becky's so young."

Talking about his cousin reminded Jack of Jan Callahan, which once again turned his thoughts toward Sheila. *God, what's my problem? Why can't I get that damn woman out of my mind?* he thought angrily.

"You seem preoccupied today. Is something wrong? Is that why you decided to come and see me?"

"No. Nothing's wrong."

"Are you sure?"

"Yes, I'm sure." Just then, his stomach rumbled. Grateful for the distraction, he pointedly looked at his watch. "It's after six."

Dorothy smiled. "You're hungry."

"Yep."

"I thought we'd go out for dinner. That okay with you?"

Now it was Jack's turn to smile. "Sure." He'd known they'd go out. His mother had never liked to cook, and now that she didn't have to, she didn't.

"You can pick the place, though."

He chose the French Quarter, a small Cajun-influenced restaurant near her house, because they had great food. Once they'd placed their orders—catfish for his mother, the crawfish platter for him—he said, "We haven't talked about your social life at all today. You dating anyone?"

She smiled. "Actually, I am."

"Want to tell me about him?"

"Sure. His name is Tom Wenger. He's an engineer, and I met him at work. He's very nice, and we've gone out a few times, and...well, there's nothing much more to tell. We're having fun together, that's all."

"Good. I'm glad. You deserve to have some fun."

"Thank you. I think I do, too."

For a few moments after that, they were both lost in thought. Then his mother looked up. "You know, Jack," she said slowly, "despite everything you've told me, I refuse to give up hope that one of these days a woman will come along who will knock all your theories about marriage and commitment into oblivion."

Jack shrugged. "Some people believe in miracles, too."

* * *

Sheila was depressed all weekend. Even seeing Jan at home and knowing she was going to be all right wasn't enough to make Sheila stop thinking about the fiasco of Friday night.

Damn you, Jack. She must have thought this one hundred times.

If only she could forget him.

A blue norther had turned Rainbow's End into a sparkling, frost-covered fairyland sometime during the night. As Sheila drove to work Monday morning she wished she could appreciate the beauty around her.

She wished…

"Dammit!" Breaking off the thought, she hit the steering wheel in frustration. "If wishes were dollars, you'd be rich. Now cut it out. For*get* him!"

She dreaded seeing Jack this morning. Bad enough he'd had that fall on Friday, but after Friday night, after knowing with certainty that he would never feel about her the way she felt about him, she wasn't sure she could manage being around him. But if she wanted to succeed at her job, she had no choice.

In addition, she also dreaded seeing Kenny. Sure, he'd been nice the other night, but maybe by now he'd had second thoughts.

She should never have gone out with him. She'd jeopardized her pleasant working relationship for the

sake of her lamebrained idea of making Jack jealous. And for what? It certainly hadn't worked.

"You'd better quit thinking about what you shouldn't have done and think about what you're going to do."

What *was* she going to do?

"You're going to go to work. You're going to act like an adult. You're going to be nice to Kenny. And you're going to ignore Jack. *That's* what you're going to do. 'Cause you're *tough!*"

She talked to herself for the rest of the way to work, and by the time she arrived, she'd just about convinced herself she could do it. Yet the moment she caught sight of Jack's silhouette, her heart tripped, and she got that stupid, hollow feeling in the pit of her stomach, and she knew it wasn't going to be easy to get through this day or any other day in his company, for that matter.

"Pitiful," she mumbled. "You're pitiful."

"Who're you talking to?"

Sheila jumped. Kenny was right behind her, and she hadn't even known it. "You caught me," she said sheepishly. "I was talking to myself."

Kenny grinned. "It's when you answer yourself that you're in trouble."

Kenny's easy smile and easier answer made Sheila feel better. Obviously, he wasn't holding Friday night against her. She returned his smile and together they headed toward the work site.

Chapter Eight

Jack saw them coming, but he pretended he didn't. He had done a lot of thinking on the drive home from Houston the night before. He had no idea why the thought of Sheila and Kenny as a couple had bugged him the way it had. It was ridiculous. Hell, if Sheila wanted Kenny, that was her lookout. As Kevin and Glenn had both pointed out, she was a big girl. She didn't need, and certainly hadn't asked for, Jack's help or his advice.

Even so, she'd better not think he was going to stand for them mooning over each other on the job, because he wasn't. There was no place on a construction site for monkey business, and he intended to let both of them know it. If they wanted to hang all over each other, they could damn well do it somewhere else.

Beckoning to Rick Clemmons to follow him, Jack headed in Sheila's and Kenny's direction. Sheila looked up at his approach, and Jack gave her a brusque "Good morning," then inclined his head toward Rick, who had lumbered up behind him.

"I'm going to be busy this morning, so Rick will be supervising you two. You're going to learn how to brace and sheath walls today."

"Okay." Kenny grinned at Sheila.

"Great." Sheila returned his smile.

"Make sure you pay close attention," Jack added, irritated by their lovey-dovey looks, "because he doesn't have time to say things more than once."

Jack knew they were probably exchanging what's-wrong-with-him? looks when he walked off, but he really didn't give a damn. He was tired of babying those two. If they wanted to work construction, then by God, they'd *work* construction without anyone holding their hands or making things easier for them.

For the next hour, he periodically checked on them as Rick set about showing them the ropes. When Jack was satisfied that Rick had everything under control, he headed toward the trailer that housed their on-site office. A couple of hours later, just as he finished making some phone calls, he saw Rick Clemmons back working with the roofers on a house two lots down from the one where Sheila and Kenny were working.

Jack frowned. Why wasn't Rick supervising them the way Jack had told him to? Hell, couldn't anyone

do anything right without him there to ride herd on them?

He slammed on his hard hat and stalked outside. Sure enough, Sheila and Kenny were working on their own, if you could call it that. Right then, they sure didn't look like they were working very hard. Sheila was doubled over laughing, and Kenny was standing there watching her with a sappy look on his face.

''You know,'' he snarled once he was within hearing distance, ''you two aren't getting paid to goof off.''

Sheila's head snapped up, and Kenny whipped around. Jack glared at her, and her face turned red. She opened her mouth, then closed it again.

Kenny said, ''Gee, Jack, we were just—''

''I saw what you were doing. You were horsing around. This isn't Pot O' Gold. I don't give a damn what you two do on your own time, but on *my* time, you're being paid to work, understand?''

''Jack,'' Sheila began, ''that's not—''

''I knew having you on this crew would mean nothing but trouble,'' he said, cutting her off again. He ignored the stunned look of disbelief in her eyes. Turning, he shouted, ''Rick! Get your ass over here.'' A heavy silence pulsated as Rick hurried to join them. ''I thought I told you to supervise these two.''

''But Jack, they were doin' great on their own,'' Rick said. ''They don't need me to watch 'em every minute.''

"I'll be the judge of that," Jack said coldly. "Unless, of course, you think you know more than I do about the job."

"No, no," Rick said, throwing up his hands. "You want me here, I'll be here."

Once again, Jack knew they were staring at his back as he walked away. Let 'em. He wasn't putting up with any garbage from anyone today. If those two wanted to play footsie, fine, but they sure as hell weren't going to do it on *his* time.

Kenny gave a low whistle once Jack was out of earshot. "Jeez, Sheila, I'm sorry. That was all my fault."

Sheila's heart was pounding, and she was so angry she could have spit. What Jack had done and said was totally unfair. She hadn't caused any trouble. She couldn't believe he'd said that. Oh, she'd like to tell him a thing or two! But as mad as she was, she knew she'd better get over it if she hoped to continue working on Jack's crew. "No, it wasn't," she muttered. "He made that pretty clear."

Rick scratched his head. "I dunno *what* his problem is. He's usually not like this."

Sheila knew what Jack's problem was. He didn't want her around, that was why he was acting like this. He'd only been nice to her last week because of Jan, but now his true feelings were coming out. Obviously, he'd decided to take off the velvet gloves and make things as hard for her as he could, even

if his treatment of her was unfair and completely uncalled for.

Well, it wasn't going to work. He wasn't going to drive her away, no matter how mean and nasty he was. She was going to succeed at this job, and she was going to make Jack Kinsella eat his words if it was the last thing she ever did.

For the rest of day Jack felt like a heel. Although he stayed away from the work area occupied by Sheila and Kenny, he couldn't rid himself of the memory of the disbelief in Sheila's eyes when he'd been berating her.

And because he was essentially a fair and honest man, he finally admitted to himself that she had not deserved to be treated that way. Hell, what had she done that was so bad? It wasn't as if she and Kenny were making out or anything. She'd just been laughing, and Kenny had been watching her. Probably, he'd told her a joke. The guys were always telling jokes on the job. It helped relieve the monotony and stress of the job and made the time go faster.

At quitting time, Jack thought about walking over and apologizing to both Sheila and Kenny, but he decided against it. She was the one who had borne the brunt of his anger, and she deserved more than an apology.

As he was driving home, he continued to think about what he could do to make it up to her. A couple of blocks from his apartment, he stopped for a red light. And there, on the right side of the street,

he saw the solution to his problem. Making a quick turn, he parked around the corner and walked to Flossie's, the local flower shop.

An hour later, armed with a dozen yellow roses, scrubbed clean and dressed in jeans and his favorite green sweater, Jack drove into the parking lot in front of Sheila's apartment complex. He'd never been there before, but he'd looked up her address in the telephone book. It was a nicer complex than the one he lived in—newer and larger.

Her unit was on the second floor. Wondering what kind of reception he'd get, Jack climbed to her level and walked toward her apartment. When she saw him, she might just slam the door in his face, he thought ruefully, and he would deserve it. He hoped not, though. He hoped she'd accept his apology and continue to be his friend.

There it was. Number 207.

He rang the doorbell.

Sheila groaned when she heard the peal of the bell. It was probably Carrie. Right now, Sheila felt too depressed to talk to anybody, even Carrie.

Maybe she'd just ignore the bell, pretend she wasn't here. But if it *was* Carrie, she would have seen Sheila's car parked in front, and she'd know Sheila was there, so she probably wouldn't go away.

Sighing, Sheila got up from the couch where she'd been lying and nursing her feelings of injury, and walked slowly to the door. She looked out the

peephole. Her heart nearly leapt out of her chest when she recognized the man outside.

Jack!

Omigod! What is he doing here?

Dozens of thoughts collided in her mind in the space of seconds. Had he come to give her another lecture? Had he decided to fire her and was going to do it in private? What?

Swallowing nervously, she smoothed down her jeans—which didn't need smoothing—and tried to calm herself.

The doorbell pealed again.

Open it. Smile. Act naturally.

She opened the door. The smile died on her face as her eyes took in first Jack, who smiled tentatively, and then the object in his hands: the most beautiful bouquet of yellow roses she'd ever seen.

Speechless, she could only stare.

"Hello, Sheila," he said softly. "I know you're probably surprised to see me."

"Um, yes..." It was all she could manage.

"I wanted to talk to you."

She licked her lips. Her brain seemed frozen. She could hardly believe Jack was there.

"Can I come in? Or are you going to make me say my piece out here?" Now his smile was self-deprecating.

"Of...of course." She took a deep breath. "I—I'm sorry. I guess I was just so surprised to see you, I forgot my manners." She stepped back.

"I'm the one who should be talking about for-

getting his manners.'' He walked in and waited until she'd shut the door behind her before continuing. ''Listen, Sheila, that's why I'm here. To apologize. What I did today...what I said...it was uncalled for. You didn't deserve it. I have no excuse. I don't know why I behaved like that. All I can say is, I'm sorry, and it'll never happen again.'' He thrust the bouquet toward her. ''I brought you these.''

Sheila could hardly take it in. She had never heard Jack apologize to anyone before. But there was no doubt in her mind that he meant what he'd said, because she could see the sincerity in his eyes. And she also saw something else. Something that chased away all the hurt feelings and replaced them with a tiny spark of hope.

Mesmerized, she took the flowers, and their hands brushed, causing her nerve endings to tingle. ''Thank you,'' she whispered. She couldn't move. Could hardly breathe. The expression in his eyes, the way he was looking at her, held her rooted to the spot.

''Am I forgiven?'' His voice contained an uncharacteristic gruffness.

She nodded. She could hear her heart beating.

''Sheila, I...''

She swallowed. ''Yes?'' Funny how she'd never noticed those little gold flecks in his eyes before.

''I...''

His gaze slowly moved from her eyes to her lips.

Sheila trembled. And then, just as she had dreamed of so often, his head dipped and slowly,

oh, so slowly, his lips brushed hers. Once. Twice. "Sheila," he said raggedly.

The flowers fell from her lifeless hands. His arms closed around her, and he kissed her again, this time slanting his mouth firmly against hers and nudging it open with his tongue. Her heart did a crazy zigzag and her knees turned to rubber as all the blood rushed to her head.

Sheila stopped thinking. All that existed at that moment were the feelings crashing through her and the stunned knowledge that the man causing them was Jack. Jack, whom she'd loved for so long.

In some part of his mind, Jack knew what he was doing was madness. But he was powerless to stop. From the second his lips had touched Sheila's the first time, he had been lost. Now the only thought in his mind was how much he wanted her.

Her lips, the warmth and sweetness of her mouth, her kisses—they were all he'd ever imagined they would be. He couldn't get enough of her, and when she returned his kisses with the same intensity and desire he felt, he knew he would never be able to stop until he'd possessed her completely.

Before long, kissing her wasn't enough, and he slid his hands under her sweater. When he cupped her breasts, she moaned, and that was all the encouragement he needed. Within seconds, her bra was unhooked and, with her help, he was pulling her sweater over her head. After that, it wasn't long

before all their clothes were discarded—thrown anywhere they landed.

He sucked in his breath at the sight of Sheila naked. She was even more beautiful than he'd imagined, and his hands trembled as he pulled her back into his arms. The feel of her skin next to his caused his heart to pump furiously. Still standing in the middle of her living room, they kissed and touched until Jack couldn't stand it anymore. He scooped her up into his arms and carried her into the bedroom. Laying her on the bed, he turned off the light.

When he turned back to her, she was smiling.

Jack's body was magnificent, but Sheila had always known it was. The work he did had honed his muscles and whittled his waist. Plus he had the most gorgeous backside she'd ever seen. Suddenly, she was doubly glad her own body was just as toned and fit as his.

The look in his eyes as he walked back to the bed caused her heart to start doing its crazy dance again. Before he joined her on the bed, he let his eyes travel the length of her body. She could see how much he wanted her, and a corresponding warmth spread through her.

She raised her arms. "Jack," she murmured.

That was all it took. Soon his body was covering hers and he began to explore all the places that cried out for his touch. But when she tried to touch him, he gently pushed her hands away.

"Not yet," he whispered.

Moving with exquisite slowness, he feathered kisses from the hollow in her neck to her stomach, then moved lower still. Sheila gasped as his mouth slowly found the place it was seeking. No, no, she couldn't stand this, she thought wildly as his tongue circled and dipped. It was torture. Delicious torture. "Please," she moaned. "Please."

"Please, what?" he murmured. "Please stop?"

"Yes. No." If he stopped, she knew she would die.

Finally, just at the point where she thought she couldn't bear another second of the tension that had built to a crescendo, her body convulsed, falling apart at its center in a release so shattering it was akin to pain.

And it was only then, when her trembling subsided and she felt like a pool of warm butter, that Jack raised himself and, taking her hand, guided her to him.

The heat and size of him shocked her—even frightened her a little—but it also excited her. She looked up into his eyes. "Yes," she whispered. "Yes."

She cried out when he entered her.

"I don't want to hurt you," he muttered.

"You're not. I want you." She raised herself up to make it easier for him to continue, because she needed him to go as deep as it was possible for him to go so that she could feel him fully. Then, and only then, would they be one. Then, and only then, would he be entirely hers.

Although she hadn't imagined she could ever feel pleasure any more intense than what she'd felt only moments earlier, this time was even better, because this time Jack was experiencing the same things at the same time. And this time wasn't just about physical pleasure. This time was about the love she felt for him, and the certainty that this union had always been meant to be.

And so when, with a shudder and cry, his life force spilled into her, Sheila exulted in the wonder and rapture, because she knew her life had changed forever.

What had he done?

Jack looked at Sheila, who was sleeping contentedly in his arms. Tenderness welled inside as he studied her. She was so beautiful. Her dark hair tumbled about her face, which looked younger and more vulnerable than when she was awake. Her skin... He swallowed. That skin. The feel of it under his fingers was forever etched into his brain. Just thinking about the way she'd felt when he touched her made him want to touch her all over again.

When she'd fallen asleep, he'd pulled the quilt that had been folded across the bottom of the bed up and over her body, but he didn't need to see it to remember every curve and every hollow.

He would never forget them.

He would never forget her.

Suddenly, he was shaken to the core. He had just made the worst, and the most irrevocable, mistake

of his life. One that would carry heavy consequences, he was sure. And yet, if he had the choice to make again, he knew he would probably do the same thing over again.

That realization, more than anything else, scared the liver out of him.

Sheila sighed and cuddled closer. She wasn't really sleeping. It was more like drifting in and out of a state of dreamy contentment. Some part of her wanted to open her eyes and wake up—to look at Jack and have him look at her—maybe even to make love again. But another part of her, the dominant part of her, wanted to keep her eyes closed forever. To stay wrapped in the cocoon and safety of Jack's arms. To never have reality intrude upon this blissful, perfect world.

"Sheila." He said her name softly, yet insistently. "Sheila, are you awake?"

Opening her eyes, she smiled up at him. "I'm awake," she murmured. She stretched a bit, then slid her arm farther around him and snuggled closer. "Um, you feel good."

"Sheila..." He moved her hand away. "I'm sorry, but I've got to go."

"Go?"

"Yes." He pulled his arm out from under her. "It's late, and tomorrow's a workday." He said it casually, as if he'd been there for a drink or something, as if they hadn't just made love.

"But..." What was wrong with him? Did he just

intend to leave? Without saying a word about what had happened between them? Did it mean *nothing* to him?

Avoiding her eyes, he walked out of the bedroom, saying, ''I'll get my clothes.''

Sheila scrambled out of bed, wrapping the quilt around her. Before she hadn't been at all embarrassed by her nakedness. Now, with the way Jack was acting, she suddenly felt ashamed. She followed him out to the living room, where he had already put on his jeans and was in the process of pulling his sweater over his head.

When he bent to pick up his shoes, she knew he was aware of her behind him. But he said nothing and continued dressing as if she wasn't there. When he was fully dressed, he finally turned to face her.

Sheila was telling herself not to be upset, but it was hard not to be. And yet she knew no matter what she really felt, she must never let him see those emotions. That would truly be the kiss of death in terms of any future relationship with him. For it was now painfully obvious to her what was going on here. Jack was scared. And he was bolting. The worst thing she could do would be try to force him into making any kind of admission or commitment to her before he was ready.

''You didn't have to get up,'' he said.

She smiled. ''I wanted to say goodbye.''

He frowned, and she could see the uncertainty in his eyes. She could almost hear the thoughts running

through his mind. Is she going to make a scene? Is she going to cry?

She laughed softly. "Come on, Jack, don't look so concerned. I'm not going to get out the shotgun. After all, I'm a big girl. What happened tonight, hey, it was great. And I wanted it as much as you did."

The relief on his face was so transparent, Sheila knew she'd convinced him.

"Yeah," he said, and now his smile was genuine. "It *was* great." He came closer, putting his hands on her shoulders. "You're one terrific lady, you know that?"

It cost her, but she managed to give him her most seductive smile. "I aim to please."

He hesitated, and in that second of indecision, she moved closer. Letting go of the quilt, she slipped her arms around his neck. If he thought he was going to make a clean getaway, he was wrong.

"Here's one for the road," she murmured, rising on her tiptoes and pulling his head down to meet hers. She poured everything she had into the kiss, and by the time it ended, he was breathing hard, and she knew he didn't want to leave.

"Now," she said breathlessly, "you'd better get going so I can get my beauty sleep." The quilt had fallen down to her feet, but she didn't reach for it. Let him look at her. Let him see what he was running away from. She stood there proudly as he awkwardly backed away.

"G-good night, Sheila."

Hearing that faint stumble as he'd said good-night

made her even stronger. "Good night, Jack." She gave him her biggest and best smile.

She kept the smile in place until he was out the door. But once it had closed behind him, she began to tremble. Wrapping herself in the quilt, she sank onto the couch and buried her face in her hands.

Jack, Jack. I love you so much.

She knew she couldn't allow herself to be hurt by his all-too-eager acceptance of her rationale for their lovemaking. If she did, he would be bound to sense it, and that would be the kiss of death. For if Sheila knew anything about Jack, she knew that when it came to women, he had a very strong sense of self-preservation.

Just be patient, she told herself. Don't crowd him or try to box him in. Just be there for him, and one of these days he'll get over his fear and see that the two of you are meant to be together.

Feeling better now, she slowly walked back to the bedroom.

Chapter Nine

Seeing Sheila every day and having to act as if nothing unusual had happened between them was tough. Real tough. Jack felt as if he were on a tightrope and that at any moment he'd make a fatal mistake and plunge off.

If only he could forget about Monday night. If only the smell of her, the feel of her, the taste of her, weren't permanently imprinted on his brain.

If only he didn't still want her.

The wanting frustrated him. Never before had a woman affected him this way. In his past life, Jack had been able to walk away from a woman without a backward glance and certainly with no regrets. But that was because he'd never been foolish enough to get involved with a woman like Sheila. His former

ladyloves had been wise to his ways. They hadn't expected anything more than he'd been willing to give.

But with Sheila...

He shook his head, disgusted with himself. What had possessed him, anyway? It wasn't as if he hadn't known he was doing something stupid when he'd made love to Sheila. He'd known, but he'd done it, anyway.

And now he had to deal with the consequences, not the least of which was the awkward position he was now in. He told himself that once he got through the first day at work, he would be fine. But he wasn't fine.

He'd dreamed about her the night before—Tuesday night—and he was just as uncomfortably aware of her today as he had been yesterday.

Any time he was in her vicinity, the atmosphere was charged with sexual tension. So charged he was afraid the other men would sense it, so he tried to stay as far away from her as he could get. But he couldn't avoid her completely, and midday Wednesday, their paths crossed as he was heading toward the equipment shed and she was returning to her work area after her afternoon break.

He had intended to give her a quick nod but found himself stopping involuntarily. Just then, a gust of wind lifted her hair. While pushing it back, her eyes met his. There was an embarrassing and unwelcome stirring in his groin, and in that moment, Jack felt like a horny kid with his first crush.

As if she knew exactly what he was feeling and thinking, she slowly licked her lips. The realization that if they hadn't been in a public place, he would have been hard put not to yank her into his arms and proceed to ravish her, shook Jack as nothing had in a long time. But even that revelation wasn't enough to stop him.

"You gonna be home tonight?" His voice sounded odd. Thick and not like him at all.

"Yes." She tucked an errant strand of hair behind her ear. "Do you want to come over?" A playful smile teased the corners of her mouth.

Damn her. She knew exactly what she was doing to him. She was doing it on purpose. He swallowed. Wished he had the willpower to say no. "Yes," he said hoarsely.

"Great." Brushing past him, she added in a low, sexy drawl, "Come early. I'll feed you."

For the rest of the day he could think of nothing else.

Sheila was ecstatic. She knew Jack was fighting against feelings that frightened him—that was pretty obvious—but he was losing. She'd been right. All she needed to do was be patient.

She stopped at Kroger on the way home and grabbed two T-bone steaks, a head of romaine lettuce, a couple of Roma tomatoes, a box of mushrooms and a loaf of freshly baked French bread. On her way to the checkout, she saw the wine and thought, what the heck. She splurged on a bottle of

good merlot. After all, she thought with a wry smile, they said all was fair in love and war.

And this was both.

At seven the mushrooms were sliced and in the frying pan along with a little soy sauce, garlic, and butter. The steaks were trimmed and waiting to be put under the broiler. The salad was made and in the refrigerator. And the table was set for two, with Sheila's nicest tablecloth and a centerpiece of the remainder of Jack's roses.

Sheila had had her shower and washed her hair. Then she'd blown it dry and left it falling naturally around her shoulders. She'd creamed herself and spritzed herself and carefully applied just a touch of eyeshadow and mascara. And then, satisfied, she'd dressed carefully, putting on a long, violet satin robe that Jan had given her a couple of Christmases ago. Under the robe she wore a matching satin teddy.

Soft music played on her CD player. All the blinds were closed and the lamps were low.

It was a perfect seduction setting, she thought in amusement. But she didn't care. She wanted Jack, and she would do whatever it took to show him he wanted her, too. Permanently.

Jack took one look at Sheila and knew he was a goner. They barely made it to the bedroom before they were making love, and this time there was very little foreplay, because he couldn't wait.

He wanted her, and he wanted her now.

He drove into her, and when she cried out, dig-

ging her nails into his back, he felt a primitive need to call out, too—a harsh and triumphant cry of possession.

His release was powerful, almost painful in its intensity, and afterward he collapsed beside her, his breathing ragged, his body completely spent.

Sheila smiled beside him. Oh, yes, he'd definitely wanted her. Satisfaction welled within as she thought about how his gaze had raked her when he saw her in the violet robe. How his eyes had darkened and his breathing had become shallow. She'd known then how much power she had over him, and she'd shamelessly used it, reaching out to touch him through his jeans and giving him her sexiest smile.

That was all it took. The next thing she knew, he had roughly pulled her into his arms and his mouth was devouring hers.

Sheila sighed. Tonight had been a fantasy come true. His tenderness and attention to detail the other night had been wonderful, yes. But she had liked—no, she had *loved*—this caveman act even more. Certainly the sex had been incomparable. Her body still tingled from the aftermath. Although she considered herself a feminist in most ways, there was something to be said for a dominant man.

Glancing at the dominant man in question, she saw his eyes were still closed. But his breathing had slowed. Testing her new power, she stroked his chest, liking the feel of the springy hair that covered

it lightly. "Hungry?" she murmured in a silky voice.

He took a deep breath and opened his eyes. "What did you have in mind?" His own voice was husky.

Sheila laughed softly. "Well...I *was* thinking about the steaks I bought...but if you're in the mood for something else..." She slid her hand lower. Her breath caught when she reached her objective. Again?

This time they went more slowly, but it was every bit as exciting because Jack was an innovative lover, and now that his first urgency had been satisfied, he determinedly set about to give Sheila pleasure. Not to be outdone, she put forth her best effort, too, and discovered it only enhanced her pleasure to make Jack feel good. Afterward, Sheila's heart felt so full of happiness, she thought she might burst.

The phone was ringing as Jack walked into his apartment.

"Hey, man, where you been? It's after midnight."

It was Kevin. Jack pushed away the guilt Sheila's brother's voice generated. "Had a hot date." It was hard to make his answer sound casual because he wasn't accustomed to lying to Kevin.

Kevin gave a short laugh. "Should have known."

"Anyway, I'm beat. What did you want?"

"You got any plans for tomorrow?"

Tomorrow. Jack hadn't even thought about Thanksgiving.

"Mom said to ask you to come and have dinner with us."

Bad idea. Real bad idea. "Tell your mom thanks, but I'm gonna pass this time."

"Pass?" Kevin said in disbelief. "Pass on Mom's turkey and stuffing? You gotta be kidding. You going somewhere else?"

"No, I've just got some stuff to take care of," Jack said evasively, wishing he'd been able to come up with a better excuse.

"On *Thanksgiving?* Whatever it is, can't it wait till the weekend? C'mon, Jack. You'll hurt Mom's feelings if you don't come."

That was the trouble with being such close friends. Kevin knew exactly which buttons to push. But Jack knew going to the Callahans' home tomorrow would be a terrible mistake. Possibly even a fatal mistake. How could he spend the day around Sheila with her family watching? Jeez, just the thought of the sex they'd shared tonight was getting him hard again. And if her family should suspect… The thought didn't bear finishing. Her brothers, Kevin included, would kill him if they thought he was messing with Sheila. He couldn't take the chance. "Look, tell your Mom I'm really sorry, but I can't make it."

It took five more minutes before Jack was able to convince Kevin that he meant what he'd said and another five of evading a straight answer on who his

date had been tonight. By the time they hung up, Jack's head was beginning to hurt.

It was starting already.

He'd always known Sheila was trouble, and here was the proof. Now Jack was lying to his best friend and having to avoid Sheila's family. If he had any brains at all, he'd end this thing before it went even one inch farther.

Sheila wasn't sure when she got the idea. It took root sometime between her mother telling Kevin how sorry she was Jack hadn't been able to come for dinner and Kevin saying Jack was the loser because she'd outdone herself this year and the turkey and stuffing were the best she'd ever made.

The idea excited Sheila, and once it was planted in her brain she could hardly wait for dinner to be over so she could put it into action. By the time she and Susan and Jan were helping with the cleanup, she was chomping at the bit. "Mom," she said casually, "do you mind if I take some leftovers home?"

"Of course not, honey. I was planning on it, 'cause your dad and I sure can't finish all of this." Rose smiled at Susan and Jan. "Do you girls want to take some, too?"

"I'd love to," Susan said. "I still haven't learned to do turkey the way you do."

"Trust me. You never will," Jan said, laughing. "And sure, Mom, I'd be glad to have some. I'm still not up to cooking."

''Are you feeling bad? You look wonderful,'' Sheila said. Seeing Jan up and about as if nothing had happened had been the best part of the day and had given them all something to be thankful for.

''I feel great,'' Jan said sheepishly. ''I'm just sick of cooking.''

They all laughed.

Rose unearthed some plastic containers, and the women began to fill them. Sheila put both white and dark meat in hers, as well as a mound of stuffing, another mound of mashed potatoes, and a hunk of cranberry sauce.

''Take some gravy, too,'' her mother urged.

A smaller container of gravy joined the rest of the food. After that, Sheila itched to get going, but she knew she couldn't leave too early. The last thing she wanted was to invite any suspicion. Finally, though, the cleanup was finished and everyone headed back to the dining room for pie and coffee. When it was over, Sheila added a piece of pumpkin pie to her stash.

Loaded down with food, she said her goodbyes and made her escape. Fifteen minutes later, pulse fluttering in excitement and anticipation, she pulled into the complex where Jack lived. She'd only been there a couple of times—riding along with Kevin when he'd picked Jack up—but she had no trouble locating Jack's apartment. She couldn't find a parking place close, though, and was forced to park around the corner from his unit. After getting out

the containers of food and locking the car, she headed for his ground-floor apartment.

His truck parked in front and the lights behind his blinds told her he was home. Delighted with herself, she rang his doorbell. A few moments later, the door swung open.

"Sheila!" He looked shocked. He also looked impossibly sexy, even dressed in faded jeans and with a day's stubble covering his chin.

"Hi," she said, grinning. "You couldn't come to the turkey, so I brought the turkey to you." She held out the containers.

He ran his hands through his hair in a distracted gesture. "I, uh, do you want to come in?"

"I thought you'd never ask." She knew he wasn't thrilled to see her, but she didn't care. Before she left, she would make him happy she'd come. Extremely happy, she vowed.

Once inside, she was pleasantly surprised to find his living room furnished attractively with an expensive-looking and beautifully designed black leather sectional sofa, slate coffee table, and contemporary wrought-iron lamps. On one wall was a light oak entertainment center with a big-screen TV currently showing a football game. Somehow she had imagined Jack living with odds and ends that didn't match, but this room reflected good taste and more. Maybe he *didn't* squander all his money. "Nice," she said, giving him an appreciative smile.

"Thanks." He seemed to have recovered his

equilibrium and reached for the containers of food. "Thanks for this, too."

"You're very welcome." To fill the still-awkward silence, she added, "If you don't plan to eat it right away, you'd better put it in the fridge."

He carried the food into his kitchen, which was separated from the living area by a waist-high bar. Sheila put her purse down and followed him. He stood with his back to her in front of the open refrigerator. Walking up behind him, she slipped her arms around his waist and laid her head against his back. "I missed you today," she said softly.

For a long moment, he didn't move. Then, gently but firmly, he removed her hands, closed the refrigerator and turned to face her. His face was troubled. "Sheila, listen, I don't know what you're thinking, but—"

She smiled innocently. "I'm not thinking anything. I meant what I said. I missed you." She dropped her voice. "Did you miss me?"

"Look, I..." Once more, he ran his hands through his hair, an unconscious gesture she now recognized as one he employed when he was disturbed. "We've got to get something straight."

The fact that he couldn't look her straight in the eyes was telling. Damning, even. And very heartening. Because Jack was a straight shooter. If he didn't care about her, he'd look her in the eyes and kiss her off without a qualm.

"I may have given you the wrong impression,"

he continued. "And if I did, I'm sorry. Thing is, I'm not interested in any kind of commitment."

"I never thought you were."

He stared at her, obviously completely at a loss by her reaction. What had he expected? That she would start to cry? Make a big scene? Oh, Jack, she thought with a rush of tender amusement, you have so much to learn about me. I'm going to be so good for you.

"You know," she said slowly, "I'm a big girl. And believe it or not, I'm not interested in any kind of commitment, either." She mentally crossed her fingers. All's fair, she reminded herself.

He frowned in confusion. "You're not?"

"Is that so surprising?"

"For a girl like you, yes."

Pretending to bristle, she said, "What's that supposed to mean? A girl like me."

"Don't play dumb, Sheila. You're not the kind of girl who sleeps around."

"No, I'm not. But that doesn't mean I'm looking for promises, either."

Studying her, he considered her answer. "No promises," he finally said.

"No promises." Sensing victory, she edged closer. "Well, Jack?" She smiled invitingly as her hands once again crept around his waist. "What do you think? Now that we've got that out of the way, want to fool around?"

"Damn you, Sheila," he muttered, but there was

no malice in the oath, just an underlying surrender that filled her with elation.

A moment later, his mouth had fused to hers.

Kevin decided he would stop by Jack's apartment on the way home. Something was niggling at him. He didn't know why, but for the first time in all the years he'd known Jack, Jack was keeping something from him, and Kevin was determined to find out what that something was.

Reaching Jack's complex, he drove through the parking areas until he arrived at the building housing Jack's unit. There were no empty parking spaces and he had to drive around the building before he found one. As he walked back toward the front, he saw a green Toyota that looked like Sheila's. Passing it, he glanced down at the license plate. Kevin blinked. It *was* Sheila's. Hmm. That was odd. He'd never heard her mention that she knew anyone who lived here. But obviously, she must. After all, he didn't know all her friends.

A few minutes later, he reached Jack's apartment. And there was Jack's truck parked in front. Good. He was home.

Kevin rang the bell.

When the doorbell rang, Jack froze with his hand on Sheila's breast. ''Who the hell could that be?'' On a sudden wave of panic, his gaze darted to the bedroom window, which faced the front of the com-

plex. But the blinds were closed. No one could see them.

"Don't answer it," Sheila said. She looked at the window, too. "They'll go away."

"My truck's out front," Jack said, lowering his voice to a whisper. "And the lights are on in the living room. Whoever it is knows I'm here."

Sheila pulled the sheet up and gave him a nervous look.

The doorbell pealed again.

"Dammit." Jack sighed in resignation. "I'd better go see who it is." Reluctantly releasing Sheila, he reached for his jeans. He hurriedly pulled them on and walked to the door. "You stay in here."

"Don't worry," Sheila said.

Even as rattled as he was by his unwanted visitor, he couldn't help noticing how sexy she looked with her hair tumbled around her shoulders and her lips all swollen from his kisses. He inwardly cursed the intruder while he yanked on his T-shirt and smoothed back his hair. Then, hoping whoever was out there could be gotten rid of quickly, he gave Sheila an I'll-hurry-back look and shut the bedroom door behind him.

His heart sank when he looked out the peephole and saw Kevin's face. Looking around quickly to make sure there was nothing in the living room to give away Sheila's presence, he finally opened the door.

"Man, it sure took you long enough," Kevin

complained, walking in without waiting for an invitation. "What were you doing?"

"I was in the can. What are *you* doing here? I thought you were gonna be at your folks'."

"I *was* there, but the party broke up early, and I decided to stop here on the way home." He looked at the TV set, which was still on. "Oh, good. You're watchin' the game." Spying the beer Jack had been drinking when Sheila arrived, he added, "Got any more of that?" Then, again without an invitation, he sank down on the couch and put his feet up on the coffee table. He obviously intended to stay awhile.

Uneasily aware of Sheila just a closed door away, and furiously trying to think of a way to get rid of Kevin, Jack headed into the kitchen to get the asked-for can of beer.

"Thanks," Kevin said, taking a long drink. "Why're you standing there? Aren't you gonna sit down?"

This was impossible. Knowing Kevin, he might park there half the night, especially since tomorrow was also a holiday for them. Alarmed, Jack recalled how many times Kevin had—after one too many to take a chance on driving home—slept on this very couch. What should he do? How could he get rid of Kevin?

Running his hands through his hair, he decided telling as much of the truth as he could was his best option. "Uh, listen, buddy, uh..." He lowered his voice and inclined his head toward the closed bedroom door. "The thing is, I'm not alone."

Kevin stared at him. "You mean...?"

Jack nodded. "Yeah. I'm, uh, kind of involved with someone new and..." Again, he gestured toward the bedroom.

"Jeez, Jack, I'm sorry." Kevin stood, his gaze going toward the closed door, too. A knowing smile tugged at his mouth. "Who is she?" he murmured. "Anyone I know?"

Hating the lies but unable to think how to avoid them, Jack shook his head.

Kevin gave him a playful punch. "Gotta hand it to you," he said. "You haven't lost the old touch." He drained his can of beer and crushed the aluminium. "Well, I'll be outta here." He grinned. "Don't do anything I wouldn't do."

Jack felt ten years older by the time the door closed behind Kevin. And all desire he'd felt for Sheila had disappeared.

He was playing with fire. He couldn't believe how close he'd come tonight to complete disaster. For if Kevin had had any inkling who the woman in the bedroom was, he would have killed Jack.

Actually, killing might be the best option Jack would face, he thought wryly, because it was a certainty that if Kevin or any other member of his family knew what was going on between him and Sheila, they would never speak to Jack again.

This thing with Sheila has got to end, he thought. *Somehow, it has got to end.*

Sheila heard most of what had been said between her brother and Jack. Certainly she'd heard enough

to know what Jack would be feeling when he came back into the bedroom. Sure enough, the expression on his face told her she'd better act quickly, before he had a chance to say anything.

Bounding up, she laughed and said, "It's about time. I was about to go crazy in here waiting for you to come back."

"Sheila, that was Kevin."

"I know."

"If he'd known you were here..."

"What are you worried about? He didn't know, and even if he did, what's the big deal?"

"Sheila, I think—"

"C'mere, big guy," she interrupted in her best Mae West imitation. She gave him a sultry look as she vamped her way to the edge of the bed. "Let's not waste any more time talking." He swallowed, his eyes glued to her as she did her impromptu little dance.

Normally, Sheila would never have been able to dance naked in front of anyone, even Jack. But she knew she was fighting for her life here. And that knowledge gave her strength.

"Sheila," he tried again. "We have to talk."

She hopped down from the bed and continued her dance in front of him. "We don't have to talk *now,*" she drawled. "Not when we have something much more fun to take care of." She pretended not to see the struggle going on within him.

For a while, his willpower remained firm enough

to resist touching her, but when she reached over and unsnapped his jeans, then caressed him, he groaned and said, ''What am I going to do about you, Sheila?''

''You're going to do exactly what you want to do,'' she said, giving him a smile filled with promise. ''Exactly what we both want.'' She pushed his jeans down and boldly stroked him.

With a raw sound of defeat, he yanked her into his arms.

Chapter Ten

Sheila and Jack had just finished breakfast, and she was cleaning up his kitchen, even though he'd told her she didn't need to bother.

"I want to," she said. "You sit there and talk to me." She indicated the bar.

"Talk?" he said, grinning. "That's a new one."

He seemed much more relaxed this morning, she was happy to note. She smiled back. "Want another cup of coffee?"

"Sure."

She poured him a fresh cup and returned to her cleanup chores.

"I've been meaning to ask you...how's Jan doing?"

"She seems to be doing great. She looks wonderful."

"I'm glad."

"Me, too." Sheila poured dish soap into the skillet and started scrubbing it. "Patrick and Jan are so close. It would have been terrible if…" She stopped, unable to finish the thought.

"Yeah," Jack agreed, grimacing. "From what I can tell, they have one of the few good marriages around." He drank some of his coffee.

Since he was the one to mention the M word, Sheila leapt on the opportunity to continue the discussion. "I'm curious. Why do you feel that way?"

"What way?"

"That there are only a few good marriages."

He shrugged. "That's simple. I have eyes."

"But I have eyes, too. And I know of a lot of good marriages. My parents, my two brothers, my cousin Jimmy, my friend Carrie's parents, practically all of our neighbors, most of the people in the choir…I could go on for hours."

"How do you know those marriages are good? You're basing your opinion on outward appearances."

"No, I'm not. I'm basing it on observing the way they act toward each other, the way they treat each other."

"Yeah, well, I'm basing *my* opinion on firsthand knowledge of my parents' and my brother's lousy marriages. Not to mention what guys say when their wives aren't around."

"Guys say a lot of things they don't mean when

they're around other guys,'' Sheila said dryly. She should know. She had five brothers.

''You could be right.'' The smile he gave her was pure Jack. ''But I don't think you are.''

The only way Jack managed to get Sheila out of his apartment on Friday was to tell her he'd promised his brother, Mike, he'd come to Austin for the weekend. Even then, she didn't want to go, and God help him, he hadn't wanted to let her go.

He couldn't get enough of her. If she hadn't been Kevin's sister, he would have kept her there the entire four days, and they probably would have spent most of them in his bed.

But she *was* Kevin's sister.

That was the whole point.

Well, maybe not the *whole* point. The whole point was, no matter what she'd *said,* he was afraid that sooner or later she would want some kind of commitment out of him. And their conversation about marriage this morning had only reinforced this fear.

''You don't really want me to go, do you, Jack?'' she'd whispered against his mouth when he'd kissed her goodbye.

Even knowing what a dangerous game he was playing, he was tempted to throw good sense out the window and worry about tomorrow, tomorrow.

Finally, she left. When the door closed behind her, he sank onto the couch. What was wrong with him? Why couldn't he end it? Hell, now she'd even reduced him to lying to *her.*

Jack groaned.

She was a witch. She'd messed with his mind.

But even as the thought formed, he knew his mind wasn't what she'd messed with. His mind knew exactly what he needed to do. It was his body that had betrayed him.

How had she managed to get under his skin this way? It wasn't as if he'd never had great sex before. What was it about Sheila that was so different and that made it so impossible for him to resist her? He groaned again, remembering how easily she had seduced him the night before. She was like a drug, and around her, he was like an addict.

Well, somehow he'd better figure out a way to conquer his addition. Otherwise he was headed down a one-way road to disaster.

Jack actually went to Austin, because he was afraid if he didn't, somehow Sheila would find out. And if she realized he'd lied to get away from her, she might also realize exactly how weak he was when it came to her.

Mike wasn't exactly overjoyed to see him, and Jack quickly realized why. The realization provided the only source of amusement he'd felt in days. It was ironic, he thought, that he should walk in on his brother the same way Kevin had walked in on him and Sheila, for Mike was entertaining a lady friend when Jack arrived Friday afternoon, and from the looks of things, Jack was going to be a fifth wheel.

"Listen, bro, I'll leave," he said quickly. "I don't want to horn in on your weekend."

Mike smiled ruefully. "No, I don't want you to go. Robin won't mind if you stay, will you, Robin?"

The lady in question, a pretty redhead with a nice smile, quickly shook her head. "Actually, I've been curious to meet you. Mike talks about you a lot." She smiled at Mike, her eyes shining with love.

Oh, oh, Jack thought. Little brother's gonna get hitched again, I'm afraid.

So he stayed. And he even said yes when Robin suggested she could invite a girlfriend to join them when they went club-hopping on Saturday night. The girlfriend, an attractive blond paralegal named Mallory was nice enough, even willing enough, but to Jack's chagrin, he had no desire to take her up on her whispered invitation to come home with her when the evening was over.

"You're spoken for, huh?" she said with obvious disappointment.

"Let's just say I'm involved and until I can get uninvolved, I'd better not complicate things."

She took the turndown like a good sport, reaching up to give him a light kiss and saying, "If you ever change your mind..."

"I'll remember that," he said.

More than anything else had, that particular episode told him just how bad things had become. As he drove home Sunday afternoon, he wrestled with the problem, but he found no solution. Maybe he would just have to let this infatuation—or whatever

it was—run its course. For surely it would. Surely he would get tired of Sheila or she would get tired of him. Yet even as he told himself that eventually this would happen, he had a nagging suspicion that in addition to Kevin and Sheila, he was now lying to himself.

Kevin was waiting for Jack when he got to the construction site Monday morning. Jack started to smile, but the expression on Kevin's face caused the smile to fade.

"I think I figured something out," Kevin said coldly.

Jack's heart gave a thump. He knew what was coming.

Kevin jabbed his index finger at Jack's chest. "You're fooling around with my sister."

Jack swallowed. He wanted to deny the accusation, but he couldn't get the words out.

"Well? Whatta you have to say for yourself?"

"God, Kevin, keep your voice down, okay?" He inclined his head toward the crew, who were just beginning to arrive.

Kevin's eyes narrowed, but he lowered his voice. "Are you serious about her, Jack?" he said tightly. "I hope so. I really hope so. Because she's not the kind of girl you mess around with if you're *not* serious about her."

"Kevin, I..." He stopped. What could he say? That Sheila wouldn't leave him alone? That he had tried to break things off, but she wouldn't listen to

him? Oh, man, he could just imagine what Kevin would say to that!

"I only have one more thing to say to you, Jack. We've been friends for a long time. But I'm going to be royally ticked if you hurt Sheila. So if your intentions aren't honorable, you'd better find a way to end this. Now."

After one last blistering look, he stalked off.

Sheila knew something was wrong the moment she saw Jack's face. He avoided her all morning, and about eleven-thirty, after telling Rick Clemmons to take over, he climbed in his truck and took off.

When he hadn't returned at quitting time, an ominous portent of dread settled into her stomach. Because she had to talk to someone and Justine was the only person who knew about her feelings for Jack, Sheila headed to the office instead of going home.

"Well, hi, Sheila," Justine said. "What brings you here?"

Sheila eyed her father's closed door. "Is he in?"

Justine shook her head. "Nope. Gone to Collins to talk to a possible new concrete supplier."

Sheila heaved a sigh. "Good. Because I need some advice."

Justine's forehead wrinkled in concern. "What's wrong?"

Sheila sank into one of the beat-up leather chairs that sat opposite Justine's desk. "I'm afraid everything's wrong." After that, the whole story tumbled

out. She ended by saying, "I'm scared. Somehow, today, the way Jack acted, I just had the feeling he's going to bolt." Tears filled her eyes. "I love him so much. And I don't know what to do."

Justine grimaced. "I really hate to tell you this, but I'm afraid you're right."

"Wh-what do you mean?"

"He was here."

"Jack?"

"Yes. He came right before lunch and went in to talk to your dad. Later, after Jack left, your dad told me to call Ed. I did, and after they talked, your dad said starting tomorrow Ed was going to take over the crew out at Willowbend and Jack was going to head up the crew in Pollero." Pollero was one of two towns that, along with Rainbow's End, made up the tri-cities area that shared the local hospital, the community college, and a dozen other facilities that would have been impossible for one town to support on its own.

Sheila's heart sank like a stone as she absorbed this news. What had happened? When she'd left Jack on Friday, everything had been fine. Oh, he'd still been a little upset about Kevin coming over, but not unduly so. She knew he'd get over it. What was different now?

"I'm sorry, hon," Justine said softly.

Sheila tried to smile, but she knew it was a pitiful effort. "I appreciate your listening."

"Anytime." Justine walked over and put her arms around Sheila.

They hugged, and Sheila could feel the tears starting again. She forced them back. "I'd better get out of here and let you get back to work."

While Sheila drove home, she thought about what Justine had told her. Tomorrow Jack was going to go to Pollero. Did he plan to call her and tell her? Or was he going to go without giving her any explanation at all? Sheila had a feeling she knew exactly what would happen once they were no longer thrown together during the day.

It's over. This is the beginning of the end.

But maybe she was overreacting. Maybe he just felt that, considering their relationship, it would be best if they didn't work together.

Oh, could that be it?

By the time she'd reached her apartment complex, she'd just about convinced herself Jack's move to the Pollero crew wasn't going to affect them at all. They would still see each other at night. After all, Pollero was only forty-five minutes away. It wasn't as if he was moving to Dallas or Houston.

When she let herself into her apartment, the first thing she saw was her answering machine blinking. Hurrying to it, she pressed the message button.

She smiled when she heard Jack's voice. She'd been right! *Call me when you get home, okay?* he said after identifying himself.

Happily, she immediately punched in his number. "Hi," she said when he answered.

"Hi. You just get home?"

"Uh-huh."

''If it's okay with you, I'd like to come over.''

''Now, you mean?''

''Yes.''

''Give me thirty minutes, then you can come.''

''All right.''

Sheila took the fastest shower on record, and by the time she heard the doorbell announcing Jack's arrival, she was clean, fragrant with her best perfume and dressed in comfortable khaki cargo pants and a black T-shirt. She hadn't bothered with a bra. If the past week was any indication, it wouldn't have stayed on long, anyway. A delicious tension trembled through her as she happily ran to the door.

''Hi,'' she said breathlessly.

''Hi.''

He looked so serious! And he made no move to come inside.

Her smile faltered. ''Aren't you going to come in?''

He nodded and moved past her.

She shut the door and told herself not to jump to conclusions. Just because he looked so stern didn't mean anything. Besides, even if he did have some idea of breaking things off, she had managed to change his mind before. She could do it again. ''Sit down, Jack. Can I get you something to drink?''

He shook his head. ''I'm not staying. I just came over to tell you something that I felt needed to be said in person and not on the phone.''

Everything in Sheila went still. And in that mo-

ment she knew this was not going to be like the other times.

"I don't think we should see each other anymore." To his credit, he looked her straight in the eye.

Sheila's heart began to pound. "I see."

"I...you're a wonderful girl, Sheila, but—"

"Is this because of what happened with Kevin? Or are you just tired of me?"

"Sheila," he said softly, and now the stern look was gone. "Does it matter what the reason is?"

"I thought you prided yourself on your honesty. Just tell me the truth. I think you owe me that much."

"Look..." He sighed. "I'm just trying to make it easier for both of us."

When it was obvious he wasn't going to say anything more, she said angrily, "Never mind. I'm sorry I asked. Actually, I understand perfectly."

"Do you?"

"Yes. You're scared, and you're running away. That's why you asked to be transferred to the Pollero crew. Well, you know what? Don't run on my account. You can stay at Willowbend. I won't make any claims on you."

"Sheila, you've got it all wrong. I'm not running away. I've never run away from anything in my life. Sure, I'm uncomfortable that Kevin has guessed what's been going on between us, but that's not the reason I think we should stop seeing each other, and it's not the reason I asked for the transfer. The rea-

son I asked for the Pollero transfer is because I thought it would make things easier for *you,* not me.''

''Kevin guessed? You mean he's talked to you about this?'' Oh, she would *kill* Kevin!

Jack nodded. ''He's not too happy about it, either. And you know what, Sheila? I don't blame him. And you shouldn't be mad at him. He was just looking out for your interests, because he knows me, and he knows I'm not the settling-down kind. And you are.''

''I don't need him to look out for my interests. I'm old enough to make my own decisions. I went into this relationship with you with my eyes wide open. I always knew what would happen in the end, so this is no surprise.'' Later, she was never sure how she managed it, but she actually gave him a smile that said she was sorry for him. ''And you know something else? I think you're the one who's going to be surprised, Jack. Because you're going to miss me. In fact, you have no idea how *much* you're going to miss me.''

''Sheila...''

He reached for her hand, but she backed away. She was strong, but she wasn't *that* strong.

He shifted uncomfortably. ''Sheila, I...I'm really sorry if I've hurt you. But the thing is, even if Kevin hadn't said anything to me, I was starting to feel an obligation here, and that just...well, it just doesn't work for me.''

''Oh, for heaven's sake. Quit making excuses.

You want out, fine. Go.'' She would not cry. She would not let him see how much he had hurt her. Walking to the door, she opened it. ''See you around, Jack.''

He hesitated, and for a moment, she thought he was going to say something else, but all he did was give her a look of regret and then he walked out the door and out of her life.

After a storm of weeping, Sheila washed her face and yanked a brush through her hair. God, she looked awful. But awful or not, she had no intention of spending the evening here, thinking and feeling sorry for herself. No man was worth it, not even Jack! she thought angrily.

Using concealer, she managed to camouflage most of the effects of her crying binge. Blusher and lipstick followed, and by the time she'd grabbed her leather jacket and headed out, she almost looked human.

But once she was in her car, she couldn't think where to go. She drove past Pot O' Gold, but she didn't really feel like spending the evening at the pub, especially not if Jack happened to come in. Eventually, she knew, she would be able to handle seeing him, but tonight everything was still too fresh.

She thought about going to China Village, her favorite Chinese restaurant, but although in the past she had often gone there alone, tonight she knew it wouldn't be a good idea.

She thought about going to see Jan, but Jan knew her too well. If Sheila did that, she'd end up telling Jan everything, and Jan had enough on her plate. She certainly didn't need Sheila's problems. Besides, it would be intolerable if the rest of her family found out about Jack. It was bad enough Kevin knew.

Thinking about Kevin, she gritted her teeth. She wished she could tell him off. But if she did that, she was afraid he would guess how much she cared about Jack, because she knew she would have a hard time keeping her true feelings hidden. Damn him. Why couldn't Kevin have minded his own business?

In the end, Sheila drove through Burger King, ordered a chicken sandwich with cheese, a vanilla milkshake and large fries—to hell with watching her diet!—and went back home, having decided that feeling sorry for herself was eminently preferable to having others feel sorry for her.

After leaving Sheila, Jack drove home, threw some clothes into his duffel and headed for Pollero. From now on, he would spend week nights at the Days Inn a few blocks from the Pollero job site. And on the weekends, he would make sure he avoided any place Sheila might be.

Anything to take him out of temptation's path…

Sheila couldn't stop thinking about what had happened and what she could have done to prevent it. The more she thought, the more upset with Kevin

she became. What gave him the right to meddle in her life like that?

At nine o'clock, no longer able to contain herself, she called his apartment. The phone rang four times before he answered.

"'lo."

"Kevin?"

"Hey. Sheila. What's up?"

She had promised herself she wouldn't raise her voice, but she could feel her good intentions fading fast. Through gritted teeth, she said, "I've got a bone to pick with you."

"What's wrong?"

"You *know* what's wrong. You stuck your nose in where it didn't belong."

For a long moment he was silent. Then, in a voice that held no hint of regret, he said, "Jack told you."

"Yes. Jack told me."

"Well, sorry about that, Sheila, but somebody had to do something."

"Why? What business was it of yours?"

"Hell, Sheila, you're my sister! How do you think I felt when I figured out what was goin' on with you two? I mean, come on. In the first place, Jack is way too old for you. And in the second place, best friend or not, I sure don't want love-'em-and-leave-'em Jack Kinsella messin' with my *sister.*"

"Just exactly what did you say to him?"

"What do you *think* I said? I told him he better have honorable intentions. I told him if he *didn't* have honorable intentions and intended to drop you

the way he drops every woman he ever gets involved with, I'd kill him. *That's* what I told him."

"Did you ever stop to think that this was not your decision to make?"

"No. I didn't. In fact, Sheila, you oughta be thanking me. You oughta be damn glad *somebody's* looking out for you, because it's pretty damn clear *you're* not. Jeez, I can't even begin to imagine what would happen if Dad ever found out about this. No telling *what* he'd do."

Sheila wanted to scream at her pigheaded brother. She wanted to tell him he'd ruined any chance she might have had with Jack. That if he'd just left them alone, things might have worked out the way she'd wanted them to.

But a sense of self-preservation prevailed. Because although she wanted Kevin to know she didn't appreciate his interference, she did not want him to know how devastated she felt. Who knew what he'd do then?

"Well, you don't have to worry about me anymore. Jack and I have decided to quit seeing each other."

"You and Jack."

"Yes."

"And that's okay with you?"

She forced herself to sigh as if she were exasperated with him. "Yes, it's okay with me."

"Then why are you mad at me for talking to him?"

"Because I don't like you interfering in my per-

sonal life, that's why. And I want your promise you won't do it again."

She was proud of herself because he seemed to believe her. Thank God, because if he had any inkling how bereft and heartsick she *really* was, he might make good on his threat to do bodily harm to Jack. And she couldn't have that. Somehow, she had to get through this on her own.

The next couple of weeks were hell for Sheila. If only she could get Jack out of her mind, but her mind simply would not cooperate. All day long, as she worked, she would remember the times they were together.

She missed him so much, and if the days were bad, the nights were worse. Some nights she only got two or three hours of sleep, and as a result, she was tired all the time.

Her work suffered. One day when she and Kenny were framing a window opening, she nailed the header to the bottom plate instead of the top plate, the way she was supposed to. Another time she neglected to bend over the nails that were sticking through the double studs.

But the worst mistake happened when she and Kenny were working on putting up a wall frame. She was the helper, and Kenny was nailing in the temporary braces. It was a windy day, and because her mind was on Jack and not on the job, she let go of the wall to extract a tissue from her jeans' pocket,

and the wall fell, tearing out the partial bracing and narrowly missing Kenny.

Ed Bassett, who had taken Jack's place, told her he wanted to talk to her. "Let's go into the trailer," he said.

Sheila knew what was coming. She even knew she deserved it. Even so, it was very hard to hear what he had to say.

"Look, Sheila," he started out, his voice kind, "is something wrong?"

Numbly, she shook her head.

"I just wondered, because you've been making a lot of mistakes lately, and it's not like you."

"I know, and I'm sorry. I promise I'll do better."

He nodded, but his gaze was thoughtful as he studied her face. "I, uh, hate to say this, but maybe you really aren't cut out for this type of work."

"No, Ed, please. Don't say that. The truth is, something *has* been bothering me, but I'll make sure it never affects my work again. And...and don't tell my father, okay? I promise you. I'll do better. I won't make any more stupid mistakes."

"*Careless* mistakes," he corrected.

"Yes, careless mistakes."

He sighed. "Okay, Sheila. I won't say anything to your father. But if anything like what happened today happens again, I won't have any choice but to let you go."

That night Sheila drove past Jack's apartment complex. She knew she shouldn't. She knew she

was behaving like a high school kid. But she couldn't seem to help herself. At the last minute, she came to her senses and didn't drive inside the gates, because if by some chance Jack should see her, she would die.

Disgusted with herself, she pointed her car toward home.

Jack worked like a demon all day, every day. He stayed at the work site for longer and longer periods of time, latching onto any excuse to keep from having to face the room at the Days Inn where his only company would be his lonely thoughts and his lonelier bed.

Being away from Sheila hadn't helped him the way he'd believed it would. He still thought about her far too much. Still remembered the times they'd been together far too vividly. And he still ached for her.

He told himself to get over it. Nothing would ever change the fact that Sheila was the marrying kind, and he wasn't. What he needed to do was start dating again. That was the quickest way to get Sheila out of his head and to begin enjoying life the way he used to.

Decision made, he gave up his room at the Days Inn, and that night, determined to conquer this weakness of his, he headed home to Rainbow's End.

Chapter Eleven

On Wednesday night, Sheila decided she could finally face the world again, so she called Carrie and asked her if she wanted to go to Pot O' Gold.

"Well, I *was* going to do my laundry, but what the heck, the laundry will wait."

Sheila couldn't help smiling. She knew Carrie would never say no to the pub because the hope was always there that she might see Glenn. Sure enough, when the two of them walked in a little before seven-thirty, Sheila spied Rory and Glenn sitting at a table near the dartboard and Kevin playing a game of darts with Joe Sullivan, the owner's son.

Trying not to be obvious, Sheila quickly scanned the rest of the pub. Relieved, she realized Jack wasn't there. She might be able to face the world,

but Jack was another story. She had heard he was staying in Pollero, but she wasn't sure if he was still there.

Just then, Rory spied them and he waved. Glenn turned around and waved, too, beckoning them over.

"Let's go say hi," Sheila said.

"Okay," agreed Carrie with a happy smile.

Sheila looked at her friend. In khaki slacks and a red twin set, Carrie looked really pretty tonight. Sheila wished Glenn *would* be interested in her.

"You guys want to sit with us?" Rory said after they'd all greeted one another.

Sheila shrugged. "Is there enough room?" The tables were small, barely accommodating four people.

"We'll shove two tables together," Glenn said.

Carrie managed to be on the other side of Sheila, so that when they sat down she ended up next to Glenn. Sheila gave an inward sigh, reminded of a line from Shakespeare: "Lord, what fools these mortals be...."

Carrie's obsession with Glenn was a case in point. Sure, Glenn was a sweetheart and very attractive, but there were other guys equally nice and equally attractive, and Carrie never gave them a second glance. Why was that? Of course, Sheila couldn't talk. She was just as bad. Here she was, pining after Jack when she could just as easily have fallen for Kenny.

We're all crazy, she decided. We want what we can't have. Well, she didn't know about Carrie, but

Sheila was determined to get over Jack. If he didn't want her, she would make herself not want him.

"Sheila, quit daydreaming. What do you want to drink?" Glenn said.

Startled, Sheila looked up and realized Kitty O'Brien was standing there. "Sorry. I guess I *was* daydreaming. I don't know. I think I'll just have a Diet Coke with a twist of lime."

Rory grinned. "My sister...the big drinker."

Kitty shrugged. "She's just got more brains than you guys."

"Now wait a minute..." Rory said in mock indignation.

Sheila and Kitty exchanged amused smiles and Sheila was reminded of the last time she'd seen Kitty and how Jack had flirted with her. Yet, for some reason, she didn't feel jealous of Kitty, which surprised her. She guessed it was because she knew the flirting hadn't meant anything. In fact, she now wondered if Jack had flirted with Kitty because he hadn't liked seeing Sheila with Kenny. The thought cheered her for a moment, but only for a moment. What did it matter why he had acted the way he had?

It's over. Stop thinking about him.

Might as well order the sun not to shine, Sheila thought with a wry smile.

Carrie ordered a Guinness, and Kitty left to get the drinks. Sheila idly turned to watch the dart game when a nearby movement caught her eye. When she

realized what it was, she nearly stopped breathing. *Jack.* Jack was heading in their direction.

Momentarily panicked, she didn't know where to look. Should she pretend she hadn't seen him? *Oh, God. I thought I could handle this, but I was wrong. I'm not ready.* By now her heart was pounding. Out of the corner of her eye, she realized he was within a couple of feet of their table. She took a deep breath and raised her eyes. Their gazes met, and for one unguarded moment, his reflected naked longing. But the emotion—if that's what it really was—was quickly banished to be replaced by his trademark lazy smile.

"Jack!" Rory said, getting up and clapping him on the back. "I thought you were stayin' in Pollero during the week."

Jack included everyone in his smiling greeting. "Living out of a suitcase gets old."

"Hey, man," said Kevin, whose game had ended. He walked over and pumped Jack's hand. "Glad you're back. We missed you."

"Speak for yourself," Rory said.

"Well, okay," Kevin said, "we didn't miss you. I was just being polite."

Everyone laughed.

The banter had given Sheila enough time to compose herself, so that when Jack said, "Hi, Carrie, Sheila," she was able to smile and return his greeting with just the right amount of casualness.

But the thought of maintaining this artificial stance for an entire night filled her with panic. It

was one thing to say hello and pretend he was just one of the guys and that his appearance hadn't devastated her, and quite another to sustain this fiction for hours.

If only he would go sit somewhere else, but she knew that was a futile hope. Of course he would sit with them. It would look too strange if he didn't. Besides, maybe she had misread that look in his eyes when he'd first seen her. Maybe he didn't care at all that she was there. Maybe, for him, what had been between them *was* just sex and she was no more important to him than any other of his discarded lovers.

As these thoughts tumbled through her brain, Kevin pulled another chair up to their table and told Jack to take a load off. Smiling easily, he straddled the indicated seat.

To keep her hands from trembling, Sheila clasped them tightly together in her lap. Thank God he wasn't sitting right next to her. That would have been unendurable. As it was, she was still much closer to Jack than she considered wise, but what could she do? She tried not to look in his direction, but she couldn't seem to help it. She wrenched her gaze away, and it landed on Kevin, who was watching her with a speculative look in his eyes. Suddenly she realized she had to be doubly careful. It was just as important to convince Kevin she had no more than a friendly interest in Jack as it was to convince Jack.

"Well, well, look who's here."

Everyone turned to look at the newcomer.

Jack smiled. "Hello-o-o, Miss Kitty. My, you sure are looking pretty tonight."

Kitty rolled her eyes. "Can it, Kinsella. I'm wise to your ways." She set Carrie's beer in front of her, served Glenn, then came around to where Sheila sat and gave her her diet drink. Returning to Jack's side, she said, "What can I get you, old silver tongue?"

Jack grinned, and everybody else laughed. Sheila did her best to join in, but it wasn't easy when her heart felt as if it were being squeezed by a giant fist.

"So how's the project in Pollero going?" Rory asked when Jack had given Kitty his drink order and she'd gone to fill it.

Sheila hardly heard Jack's answer because she was so miserably aware that the evening had just begun and there was no way she could endure hours of this. Yet there was no way she could leave. If she'd been alone, she might have been able to think of some excuse to get out of there, but she wasn't alone, and if she said she wanted to go, Carrie would throw a fit. Not to mention what her brothers would think and say. And Jack...oh, God. If he were to suspect why she was leaving...that simply didn't bear thinking about. No. She would have to stay at the club for a reasonable length of time. But just because she couldn't go home didn't mean she couldn't have a temporary reprieve.

"I'm going to the ladies'," she mumbled to Carrie, nearly knocking her chair over as she grabbed

her purse and hastily got up. She didn't wait for Carrie's answer.

Once in the rest room, Sheila put her hands over her feverish face. Tremors shook her body as she fought the tears that were so close to overflowing, she almost couldn't stop them. Yet somehow she did. Somehow she found reserves of strength she hadn't known she possessed. Somehow she forced herself to breathe deeply and slowly until her body quieted and her heart slowed.

"You can do this," she whispered. "You *will* do this. You *must* do this."

Five minutes later, head high, face determinedly unruffled, she walked out of the rest room and back to the table. She might not have Jack, but she still had her pride, and she would hang on to that with every ounce of strength in her body, no matter what else happened tonight.

Jack didn't want to watch her coming, but he seemed incapable of looking anywhere else. Like a magnet, Sheila pulled his gaze.

God, she was beautiful. Tonight she wore some kind of body-hugging pants—he thought they called them leggings—in navy blue or black, it was too dark to tell, paired with a long white sweater. On anyone else, the outfit probably wouldn't be considered sexy, but in Jack's opinion, anything Sheila put on was sexy.

Her clothing sure didn't disguise that body of hers. His groin tightened just thinking about her

body. He gritted his teeth. What was wrong with him that he couldn't stop wanting her? It was as if she'd bewitched him. Maybe she *was* a witch, he thought in wry amusement, because she certainly had cast a spell on *him.*

In fact, right now what he wanted most in the world was to get up, sweep her off her feet and into his arms and carry her out of there and straight to his apartment, where he would make love to her so thoroughly she would never want to leave.

Never want to leave?

Wait a minute. Wait just a minute. Where had *that* thought come from? Since when did he want a woman around permanently?

He took a long swallow of his beer. Reminded himself of his dreams and plans. The early retirement. The boat. The carefree, no ties-, no responsibilities-lifestyle he had saved and sweated for.

His goals hadn't changed. He still wanted that. So no matter how much he burned for Sheila, no matter how much he missed her—he had made the right decision in cutting her out of his life.

In fact, it was because he burned for her and missed her so much that he knew how right that decision was.

Never forget it, buddy, she's the marrying kind. And you're not.

Telling himself he had had a narrow escape and was damn lucky he'd come to his senses in time, he returned his attention to his drink and his buddies,

neither of which would ever make any demands on him.

As the night wore on, Sheila found it harder and harder to keep laughing and pretending she was having a good time. It became especially hard when Jack began to flirt with Kitty again. That Kitty didn't take him seriously and that it was obvious he didn't, either, made no difference. It still hurt to see him put his arm around Kitty and laughingly pull her onto his lap.

The final straw came when he asked Kitty what time she got off work.

''Too late to want anything other than to fall into bed,'' Kitty said, laughing and evading his hand, which had reached out to pat her behind.

''I've got a bed,'' he drawled.

That did it. Sheila might be strong, but she wasn't a masochist. ''Speaking of bed,'' she said, ''I'm a working girl, and I'm beat.'' She stood. ''Carrie, if you're not ready to leave yet, maybe one of the guys will give you a ride home.''

''Well, I...'' Carrie looked hopefully at Glenn. ''Would you mind?''

Sheila felt kind of bad about putting Glenn in this position, but not bad enough. After all, brother or not, Glenn was a man, and right now she didn't feel kindly toward any member of the male species.

''Nah, that's okay. I can give you a lift,'' Glenn, always the gentleman, said.

Sheila smiled brightly, looked around the table,

said a general good-night to everyone without actually looking anyone directly in the eyes, and left. When the front door closed behind her, she vowed she would never go back.

Jack left soon after, telling Kitty since she wouldn't go home with him, he had nothing to look forward to, so he might as well leave. They both knew he wasn't serious.

"Got a long drive ahead of me tomorrow," he said by way of explanation to Kevin, who looked at his watch and raised his eyebrows.

Jack couldn't admit, even to himself, that Sheila's departure had plunged him into gloom, just as if a light switch had been turned off. Suddenly he had no desire to sit there. No desire to drink beer. No desire to yuck it up with the guys. And no desire whatsoever to continue flirting with Kitty.

Maybe he should have stayed in Pollero, because it was becoming more and more obvious to him that the consequences of his involvement with Sheila were more far-reaching than he'd ever imagined they would be.

Over the next two weeks Sheila spent most of her free time getting ready for Christmas. More than any other time of year, Sheila loved Christmas. The crisp weather—sometimes they even had snow—and the excitement in the faces of all the children, the Christmas carols playing everywhere, the holiday

decorations, but most of all, the feelings of peace and goodwill that seemed to pervade everything.

This year, though, it was hard not to slide into depression, because another thing about Christmas was how aware a person was when they had no one with whom to share the beauty and joy of the season.

Of course, the minute she thought that, she realized how untrue it was. She had a large and loving family and many, many friends.

"Count your blessings," she chided herself each time she started feeling sorry for herself.

Christmas fell on a Friday this year, and Sheila's father gave everyone Thursday and Friday off with pay. Sheila spent Thursday wrapping presents and trying to decide what she would wear Saturday night. Jan and Patrick, who were celebrating Jan's recovery, were having an open house.

Sheila was looking forward to it, because she'd found out—in a roundabout way—that Jack wouldn't be there. Supposedly he was spending the entire weekend in Houston with his mother. She wasn't sure what she would have done if he had been going, because nothing short of a catastrophe would have been an acceptable excuse for her missing the party, and she still wasn't sure she could have handled being in his company for an entire evening.

After going through her entire wardrobe, she finally settled on a black crepe dress she'd bought the year before to wear to a friend's wedding. The dress

was simple, with cap sleeves, a jewel neckline, and a modest body-skimming design that ended several inches above the knee. Now, if Jack were going, she might have chosen a sexier outfit just to remind him of what he'd thrown so callously away, she thought angrily.

She liked it when she could feel angry with him, because anger was infinitely preferable to the aching sadness she sometimes succumbed to.

Sheila spent Thursday night with her family—the time when they traditionally exchanged their gifts. Her parents stunned her with theirs: a gorgeous pair of diamond earrings.

"I don't know what to say. They're so beautiful." She was all choked up.

They were equally generous with the rest of the family. Her dad shrugged off the thanks, saying the company had had a very good year.

Sheila and her brothers had all gone in together to give their parents a Caribbean cruise.

"A cruise!" her mother said. She looked at Sheila's father. "Patrick! We're going on a cruise." She was clearly delighted.

Sheila and Keith, whose idea the cruise had been, exchanged congratulatory looks, although Sheila wasn't sure her father shared her mother's sentiments. Patrick, Sr., would have been content to never leave the confines of Rainbow's End. He'd be a good sport, though, and he'd probably enjoy the trip once he was actually there.

On Christmas Day the clan gathered again—this

time for dinner in the afternoon. This year Susan's former mother-in-law Laverne Sheridan was included as well as Sheila's Uncle Sean and his wife.

Every time Sheila looked around the table, she was reminded of the year before, when Jack had been with them, too. But she refused to dwell on the past, especially on what might have been. She was determined not to let her persistent melancholy over Jack ruin her holidays, and for the most part, she was successful.

On Saturday, Sheila went to the health club in the morning and spent the afternoon cleaning her apartment. She'd promised Jan she would arrive early so she could help with last-minute preparations for the party, so at four-thirty she started getting ready.

At six-fifteen she parked her Toyota in Jan's and Patrick's driveway, then walked to the back door, where she let herself in without bothering to knock.

"Oh, great, Sheila, you're just in time," Jan exclaimed when Sheila walked into the kitchen. "By the way, you look fabulous."

"Thanks, so do you."

Jan wore a crimson velvet dress that Sheila recognized as her matron-of-honor outfit from Susan and Keith's wedding.

"What do you want me to do?" Sheila asked.

"Aprons are in the pantry," Jan said. "Do you mind putting the ham on that platter over there?" She inclined her head toward a spiral-sliced ham sitting next to an oblong crystal platter.

Sheila smiled obligingly and was soon working

alongside Jana, who was filling deviled eggs, and Katie, who was arranging crackers around a bowl of dip.

"So how many people are you expecting?" Sheila said.

"About sixty altogether."

"Wow."

Jan laughed. "I know. It'll be a real houseful. I imagine the peak time will be about nine." The party was scheduled from seven till eleven.

Sheila looked at the clock. The early birds would begin arriving soon. Sure enough, a few minutes before seven, the first guests rang the doorbell. "Jan, you go on out there and greet people. We'll finish up here."

By seven-fifteen all the food was ready and out on the dining room table, so Sheila felt free to circulate and say hello to the early arrivals, among whom were her parents. Until about eight, a steady stream of people—including most of the remainder of Sheila's family—joined those already there, then there was a slowdown. But about eight-forty-five, the doorbell rang again.

Sheila was closest to the door so she signaled to Patrick that she'd get it. With a warm, welcoming smile, she opened the door. And nearly fainted. For standing on the stoop was the man who had occupied the lion's share of her thoughts the past few weeks.

"H-hello, Jack." She knew she must look

stunned to see him, but it was such a shock. He wasn't supposed to be there.

"Hello, Sheila. Merry Christmas."

Heart thudding so hard she was afraid he'd hear it, she stood back to let him enter. Unfortunately for her, he looked unbelievably good. Wearing charcoal slacks paired with a dress shirt and tie only a shade lighter and a black wool sport coat, he could have stepped out of the pages of a men's magazine. As he walked inside, she got a whiff of his cologne—something clean and woodsy—and it did something to her insides.

Still trying to compose herself, she searched frantically for something to say. "I didn't think you were coming." Oh, God. Why had she said that? Now he'd know she'd been thinking about him.

"I decided to drive back to Rainbow's End this morning. I felt kind of like a fifth wheel in Houston."

"Fifth wheel?"

"Yeah. My mother has a gentleman friend, as she puts it." His smile was fond. "And he seems to be monopolizing her time. Not that she's complaining."

"Well, I know Jan and Patrick will be glad you could make it." There. She'd finally managed to sound cool and relaxed, just as if the sight of him hadn't shaken her to her very center. "They're over there." She pointed in Patrick's direction. "If you'd like a drink, the bar's in the kitchen, and the food is in the dining room." She desperately wanted to

get away from him, but she wasn't sure how to do it without being obvious.

"Thanks."

Sheila wondered if he felt uncomfortable, too. He seemed subdued tonight, and the way he was looking at her was making her even more discombobulated.

After a few more awkward moments passed, Sheila was finally saved by her cousin Jimmy, who walked over and clapped an arm around Jack's shoulders.

"Jack!" he said heartily. "Haven't seen you in a long time. Where you been keepin' yourself?"

As Jack turned to answer, Sheila mumbled a hasty "Gotta check on the food" and made her escape.

"Was that Jack I saw come in?" Jan said when Sheila entered the dining room.

"Yes." Sheila explained what he'd told her.

Jan smiled. "I'm glad he could make it. I've always liked Jack."

"Yes. Me, too." Sheila was proud of herself. She sounded quite normal.

"You know..." Jan frowned. "Even more so than your bachelor brothers, I've wondered why Jack has never married. He'd make such a great husband, I think."

For some idiotic reason, this innocent comment caused tears to burn at the back of Sheila's eyes, and it was a second before she felt steady enough to answer. "He's made no secret of the fact that he doesn't believe in marriage."

Jan shrugged. "I know. But I just don't believe he really means what he says. I think that front he puts on is bluster, pure and simple. A defense mechanism. Lots of guys do that to cover up the fact they are really softies underneath and are afraid of getting hurt."

Still fighting the urge to cry, Sheila said a noncommittal "Maybe." *But in the process, they sure do hurt the women who are fool enough to fall in love with them.*

"Well, I think I'll go say hello to him," Jan said.

Sheila nodded. She was angry with herself. Somehow she was going to have to master her emotions. She simply couldn't keep falling to pieces every time Jack was anywhere in her vicinity. "Where's your pride, girl?" she muttered under her breath.

As she busied herself replenishing some of the platters of food—all the while lecturing herself—she managed to regain her equilibrium. And by the time she rejoined the group in the living room, she was determined not only to get through the rest of the evening without incident but to enjoy herself in the process.

Jack knew it was the height of folly to have come to the party. But no matter how many times he'd told himself this, he hadn't been able to stay away. The truth was, he'd wanted to see Sheila.

And now that he was here, he could hardly tear his eyes away from her, even though he knew it was best for both of them if he gave her a wide berth.

He wondered if she knew how desirable she looked tonight. He never would have believed a dress as simple as the one she wore could be so sexy, but the fact that it only hinted at the delectable body it covered was more of a turn-on than a more revealing outfit would have been.

Finally, he could stay away from her no longer, and he joined the group she was talking to. Only the barest flicker in her eyes betrayed her awareness of his presence. The others greeted him warmly—he knew just about everyone in the room—and asked him about the Pollero project. There were no secrets in Rainbow's End, he thought in amusement. Everyone knew everyone's business, and that was both the weakness and the strength of living in a town like this. You had no real privacy, but you also had an incredible support network.

After that subject was exhausted, one of the women asked Sheila about her job. "I couldn't believe it when I heard you'd joined one of the crews," she said, wrinkling her nose. "Whatever for?"

Jack couldn't help feeling a ripple of pride as Sheila coolly explained her reasons. She was some kind of woman, he thought. Feminine and sexy, but strong and tough, too. She didn't take guff from anyone.

"But surely," the woman persisted, "you don't want to do manual work forever? I mean, I can understand how you might have something to prove,

but...'' She broke off, obviously genuinely perplexed.

''I intend to work construction as long as they'll have me,'' Sheila said.

''That means she'll be there as long as she likes,'' Jack said, ''because she can hold her own alongside any of the men.''

Sheila looked at him in astonishment.

''What?'' he said. ''It's true.''

''I know it's true. I just never thought I'd hear you admit it.''

They all laughed. When the laughter subsided, Jack said, ''I always admit when I'm wrong.''

''A man who can admit he's wrong,'' said another of the women. ''Wow. I envy the woman who finally lands you, Jack.''

Although his standard reply to this kind of remark was usually a flippant ''I wouldn't hold my breath if I were you,'' or something similar, tonight he just smiled crookedly and let the statement pass without comment. It took all his willpower to keep from looking at Sheila, but he was acutely aware of her beside him.

And in that moment of truth, he finally admitted to himself that it wasn't going to be as easy as he'd imagined to forget her.

Chapter Twelve

Kenny asked Sheila if she had plans for New Year's Eve.

She smiled. "I always go over to my parents' house. We play games like Trivial Pursuit. It's kind of corny, but it's fun. What about you?"

He shrugged. "I don't really have any plans."

Impulsively, she said, "Why don't you join us? It's not a wild party or anything, but I think you'd enjoy it."

"But it's just your family..." His expression seemed wistful.

"Actually, my friend Carrie—you met her that night at Pot O' Gold, remember?—is coming, too, and I think one of Glenn's friends will be there." She grinned. "The Callahans always have hangers-on."

"In that case, thanks. I'd like to come."

Sheila hoped Kenny realized that her invitation was only a gesture of friendship, but she didn't really worry about it, because he seemed to take it in that spirit.

The evening turned out to be one of the nicest of the entire holiday season. The fact that Jack wasn't there—as he had been the year before—helped. Sheila really enjoyed herself, and Kenny seemed to, too. In fact, about halfway through the evening, Sheila realized he was showing more than a passing interest in Carrie. And wonder of wonders—Carrie seemed to be reciprocating. Sheila hoped her interest in him wasn't feigned as a ploy to make Glenn notice her.

The following day, when Carrie called, Sheila came right out and asked her.

"I really like Kenny," Carrie confessed. "A lot. In fact, that's why I'm calling. He...he asked me out, but if you mind, I won't go," she added in a rush.

"Why should I mind? I'm delighted he asked you out." Yet Sheila couldn't help feeling a twinge. It sure hadn't taken Kenny long to get over her, she thought ruefully. Combined with Jack's rejection, she was batting a thousand in the uninterested beau department.

Within weeks, Carrie and Kenny were an acknowledged couple. It was a bittersweet experience for Sheila to see the shining happiness on Carrie's

face, for it reminded her all too poignantly of what was missing in her own life.

One night toward the end of the month when Sheila was feeling particularly low, she decided maybe she needed a change of scene. January was such a depressing month, anyway. The weather in Rainbow's End was usually chilly and rainy, and this year was no exception, plus there was always a letdown after the holidays.

Maybe she should go visit her cousin Maggie. Maggie was Sheila's Uncle Sean's daughter, and even though she was ten years older than Sheila, the two had always been kindred spirits. Maggie lived in New York. She was a successful theatrical agent and had a glamorous job and an apartment in a brownstone near Central Park. For years she'd been inviting Sheila to come and stay with her.

Yes, Sheila thought. That's exactly what I'll do. She had some vacation coming to her, so why not take it? Suddenly excited, she jumped up to go and look at the calendar. She rolled her eyes as she realized she still hadn't changed over to the new one. While taking down the old calendar, her eye fell on a notation that gave her a jolt. On the square for December 10, she'd put a little red X in the bottom right-hand corner—her private symbol for the day she was due to start her period.

She swallowed.

And stared at the X.

Another thing she always did was put a circle around the X to keep track of when her period ac-

tually showed up. That way she counted accurately to forecast the next month.

There was no circle around the X for December 10.

Dear God.

Her heart beating like a bass drum, she licked suddenly dry lips. She felt frozen and could hardly comprehend what her eyes were telling her. Slowly, she turned the page back to November. Sure enough, there was the circled X on November 14.

And now it was the third week of January.

I've missed two periods.

The realization was devastating. There could only be a couple of reasons for missing two periods. Either she had some horrible disease or she was pregnant.

She sank into the nearest chair. She knew she wasn't sick. In fact, physically she'd never felt better. Her body had finally become accustomed to her new job, and except for occasional soreness when she used muscles that she hadn't used much before, she felt strong and fit.

Her breasts had been tender lately, though. She'd noticed the tenderness when she'd showered, but she hadn't thought anything of it.

Now she understood.

She was pregnant.

With Jack's child.

How was it possible? Every time she and Jack had been together, he had used a condom. Even that first time, when she knew he hadn't come to her

apartment with sex in mind, he had been prepared. In fact, she'd teased him about it, saying something like, ''Do you always carry condoms around with you?''

He hadn't been embarrassed by the question and had answered in a way she couldn't fault, saying seriously, ''I believe in protection.''

Unspoken was the fact he'd also believed in being prepared. With his aversion to marriage, Jack was taking no chances. Sheila had understood that, and even though the knowledge saddened her personally, on a practical level she appreciated his prudence.

Yet the fact remained. Despite his precautions, she was pregnant.

Condoms aren't one hundred percent foolproof. Hadn't she read that somewhere?

Oh, dear heaven, what was she going to do?

All thoughts of going to New York were discarded. Sheila knew the trip would be wasted on her now. For the next two weeks, all she could think about was her pregnancy, which she confirmed with a home pregnancy test. She'd had to drive to Hilltop to buy the kit because she didn't dare do it in Rainbow's End...or even Pollero, for that matter. Good grief, what if she should run into Jack?

Her hand shook when she stared at the results of the test. Yes, she'd known from the day she looked at the calendar, but a tiny, secret part of her had hoped she was wrong.

Today she knew, without a doubt, she wasn't wrong.

Despite everything, part of her was elated. She was going to have a baby. Jack's baby. She touched her stomach with tears in her eyes. She and Jack had made this baby. She would have a part of him forever.

Over the next weeks, her emotions seesawed between happiness and despair. The despair was caused by the shock and disappointment she knew her parents would feel when they found out. In spite her father's pigheadedness in regard to Sheila working on one of the crews, she knew he was very proud of her. And a great deal of that pride came from the fact that Sheila, like so many of their friends' children, had never done anything to cause her parents embarrassment or pain.

She grimaced. Her father probably thought she was still a virgin. He belonged to the old school of thinking, the one that said nice girls didn't. In fact, her father probably preferred to think she didn't even *know* about sex. She chuckled at the thought, but there was an undercurrent of pain in her amusement. Her father's regard meant a lot to her, and it hurt her to realize that once her father knew about the baby, she would slip in his estimation. Yes, he would still love her and he would do everything he could to help her, but he would never again think of her in quite the same way. *I'm not sure I can bear it.*

And Jack.

What would her parents and brothers say about Jack? They would be furious. They would never forgive him. He would be an outcast.

And all this anger and pain could be avoided if only Jack loved her.

Sheila smiled ruefully. If only. Were there ever two sadder words? If only Jack loved her. If only she could proudly tell her parents. If only she and Jack were getting married. Then the news about the baby wouldn't be so hard for her parents to accept, even if the birth came months earlier than it should. They could still hold their heads up among their friends, for Sheila certainly wasn't the first daughter to put the cart before the horse.

But Jack *didn't* love her.

And they weren't getting married.

But what if Sheila told him about the baby? She wanted to. Oh, God, she wanted to, even though he'd made his feelings about kids quite clear, too. But surely, if he knew, his feelings would change. After all, thinking about kids objectively and thinking about a child already conceived were two very different things.

But as tempting as it was to tell him, she couldn't do it. Yes, he would probably do the right thing and marry her. But Sheila didn't want him out of a sense of obligation. She wanted him to come to her freely, because he loved her and needed her and wanted to spend the rest of his life with her.

Oh, Jack, it could be so wonderful. Why don't you love me? Tears brimmed in her eyes, and she angrily

wiped them away. She couldn't waste any more energy crying over him. He didn't love her, and that was that. She had to face it and move on, because now she didn't just have herself to consider. She had a baby coming the end of August.

Yet if she stayed in Rainbow's End, Jack *would* find out about the baby. After all, it wasn't as if she could hide her pregnancy. What then? Wouldn't he figure out he was the father? Did she want that? And if she didn't, what was the alternative? The only way to keep Jack from finding out would be to leave Rainbow's End...and soon. Before her pregnancy was evident. And if she did that, would she even tell her family? Or would she try to hide the pregnancy from everyone? But what would happen after she had the baby? Did she want to give it up for adoption?

Sheila swallowed.

No. Everything in her screamed the word. No. This was her baby. Hers. She was keeping it.

All through February and most of March, Sheila wrestled with the problem and how to handle it. She couldn't seem to come to any decision, yet she knew her time was quickly running out. She was nearly four months pregnant, and even though she wasn't yet showing, she soon would be. As it was, she'd gained six pounds and had had to buy a bigger size in jeans. She also now wore her shirts untucked. So far, no one had commented. But she knew people had noticed. Or maybe they hadn't. Maybe she was

just so aware of the differences in her body, she figured everyone else must be, too.

Actually, most people were so self-involved, they didn't notice changes in others until those changes were so glaringly apparent, they could no longer be ignored. Susan and Jan were two cases in point. Susan was blissfully waiting for the birth of her new baby, which would happen in late May. Everything else was viewed through rose-colored glasses. And Jan's entire energy was completely concentrated on her health right now, and rightly so. Then there was Carrie, who was so caught up in being in love she didn't know anyone else besides Kenny was alive.

One rainy Sunday night at the end of March Sheila lay in bed with her hands on her stomach and listened to the wind and the spatters of rain against the windowpane and thought about the possibility of going to New York to live with Maggie. She knew Maggie would take her in. And Sheila had enough in savings to carry her through the birth of the baby and a few months afterward.

But then what? Would she stay in New York? Would she tell her family about the baby? She finally fell asleep, her decisions for the future still unresolved.

The next day, on the job, she was so preoccupied she stepped into a hole and fell and twisted her ankle.

"Sheila!" Kenny said, racing to her side. "Are you okay?"

"Yes, I'm fine." Embarrassed, she shrugged off

his help. As they both went back to work, she realized that continuing to work on the construction crew was probably not the smartest thing for her to do. Her father and brothers had been right. The work *was* dangerous. It might be different if she was an old hand at the job, but she wasn't. She was a rookie and still learning. What if she had a serious accident? What if she harmed her baby?

But if she were going to stay in Rainbow's End, she had to support herself. Later, as she was eating her lunch, she thought about the possibility of going back to work in the office. Wryly, she thought how happy her father would be if she told him that was what she wanted to do. Of course, when he discovered the reason for her change of heart, he wouldn't be happy for long.

But how could she do that? If she went back to the office, Justine would no longer have a job. And Justine loved the job, plus she was better at it than Sheila had ever been. So going back to the office was not an option.

That left New York.

Jack finally figured out how to stop thinking about Sheila. The answer was work. From January through March, he worked at least twelve hours a day. Counting the near-hour it took him to get to Pollero in the mornings and the near-hour it took to get home at night, he used up most of the day.

Nights were still difficult, because his memories

of her were pesky and refused to go away, especially once his body was relaxed.

But he was determined, and where there was a will, there was a way, he reminded himself. He *would* get over Sheila. It was just a matter of time.

The day after Sheila's fall, she called Maggie.

"Sheila! How great to hear from you," Maggie said happily.

Sheila had always been envious of Maggie's voice. It was wonderfully husky and sexy. A bedroom voice, Kevin called it. Maggie also had bedroom eyes, dark blue and rimmed with thick black lashes. But there was nothing sexy or bedroom oriented about Maggie's personality. She was smart, determined and ambitious, with a no-nonsense quality about her that made you feel you could trust her with anything.

"Are you finally coming to visit me?"

"Well, that's why I was calling. I..." Sheila stopped. Before placing the call, she had decided she would tell Maggie everything. Now that the actual moment of truth had arrived, Sheila was finding it harder than she'd imagined. She took a deep breath. "I'm thinking about coming, but first I'd better tell you why. Then you can tell me if you still want me."

Ten minutes later, Sheila ended her story by saying, "So now you know."

"Sheila, I don't have to think about this. Of course, you're welcome. Come and stay as long as

you like. I have an extra bedroom, and as long as you don't mind sharing it with the baby after it's born, I don't mind you being here."

"But won't I cramp your style?" Sheila envisioned Maggie with an active social life that probably included a lover or two.

Maggie chuckled. "You mean my fourteen-hour days at the office? No, you won't cramp my style. I'd love having you. Hey, can you cook?"

Sheila grinned. "I'm not a gourmet, but I can make meat loaf and spaghetti."

"You're hired."

"Oh, Maggie, thank you. I can't tell you what this means to me."

"What about your parents? What do you plan to tell them?"

"I don't know," Sheila confessed. "I hadn't gotten that far in my thinking. First I wanted to make sure this was okay with you."

"It's more than okay with me. You know what? You'll probably laugh about this, but I actually miss being around family. I never thought I'd say that, but lately, I don't know. Maybe it has to do with getting older or something."

There was a wistful quality to Maggie's voice that surprised Sheila. She'd always thought of her older cousin as a woman who had known what she wanted from life and who was unqualifiedly satisfied with her choices.

"Leaving my family is the hardest part of this for

me,'' Sheila said. ''But having you to be with will make it a lot easier.''

''Sheila, it'll be such fun to show you New York. And I think you'll love it here. There's so much to do. So much to see.''

Sheila smiled. Maybe it *would* be okay.

''When do you think you'll come?'' Maggie asked.

''I'm not sure.'' The company picnic was taking place Saturday. For some reason, Sheila didn't want to tell her parents before then. ''I'll talk to my parents on Sunday. Then I'll call you, okay?''

''Okay.''

After they hung up, Sheila stared at the phone. The die was cast. Now the only decision left was whether she would tell her parents the true reason she was making this move.

Jack had been trying to decide whether he would attend the company picnic. He'd never missed one, and he didn't want to miss this one, either, but he wasn't sure it was a good idea to see Sheila.

Yet when Kevin called him on Thursday night to remind him to bring his bat and glove, Jack found himself agreeing to get to the park early so they could get in some practice for the annual softball game.

''I'm determined to beat Patrick's team this year,'' Kevin said. ''I'm counting on that fast ball of yours.''

So the question was settled. Jack was going to the

picnic, and ready or not he would see Sheila again. He told himself he would handle it. Who knew? Maybe enough time had passed that he would find she no longer had the power to affect him.

Since talking to Maggie on Monday night, Sheila had thought and thought about what she would tell her parents. She had finally decided nothing less than the truth would suffice. She had never lied to them, and she wasn't about to start now.

Once that decision was made, she felt ten times better. She actually slept well on Thursday night.

Then on Friday, something happened that threw everything she'd decided into chaos. She had just gotten off work and was heading for her car when Ed Bassett poked his head out of the office trailer and called to her.

''Phone call,'' he shouted.

Frowning, Sheila changed direction and made for the trailer. Who would be calling her at work? It could only be someone in the family. Concerned now, she hastened her steps.

''It's Patrick,'' Ed said. ''Your brother.''

Really concerned now, Sheila took the phone. ''Patrick?''

''Sheila, I'm glad I caught you. Could you stop by here on your way home?'' His voice sounded strained.

''Wh-what's wrong?'' Sheila said.

''Jan got bad news today,'' he said in a lower

voice. "She's upset." His voice cracked. "I—I need you here."

Heedless of how grimy she felt, Sheila said without hesitation, "I'll be there in fifteen minutes."

Although she wanted to get to Jan's and Patrick's as quickly as possible, she observed the speed limits and took no chances on the way. She had the baby's welfare to think about now, not just her own. As she drove, she told herself not to think the worst. But Patrick had said bad news. That must mean Jan's cancer had reappeared. Yes, Sheila was sure that must be what had happened, for she remembered Jan mentioning earlier in the week that she would have her first follow-up X ray today.

"She's in our bedroom," Patrick said when Sheila got to the house. His eyes were red-rimmed, and Sheila knew he'd been crying. This more than anything told her of the seriousness of what they'd found out, for Patrick was the most stoic of her brothers. In fact, she could never remember him crying before.

Sheila knocked softly on the bedroom door. Jan's muffled voice said to come in.

Jan was sitting on the side of the bed. When she saw Sheila, her face crumpled. A moment later, they were holding each other tightly. Jan was crying, and Sheila's own eyes spilled over. Finally, Jan drew a shaky breath and loosened her grip.

"I'm sorry," she whispered. "I'm just so frightened."

"Tell me," Sheila said.

And so Jan did. She'd gone into Austin that morning. Patrick had wanted to go with her, but she told him not to be silly. "It's just a follow-up," she'd said. She'd had the X rays and waited in Dr. Vogle's office for the results. The radiologist had called him while she was there. She could tell from Dr. Vogle's reaction that the news wasn't good. Minutes later the X rays themselves were delivered to Dr. Vogle. He'd been gentle when he'd told her—and later shown her—what they revealed.

"Two more lumps," Jan said, her eyes meeting Sheila's. "In the other breast."

"But that's not *that* bad, is it? I mean, didn't he say before that there was a chance you *would* develop other lumps?"

Jan swallowed and nodded. "Yes," she said bitterly, "but what he *didn't* say was what would happen if I did." She closed her eyes. "He's recommending a double mastectomy and even more aggressive radiation afterward."

Oh, God. Sheila had a guilty urge to touch her own breasts. To make sure they were still there, whole and healthy. Instead, she put her arms around Jan again.

Once they both had themselves under control, Sheila asked if a double mastectomy was really necessary. "Don't you think you should have a second opinion? Maybe even a third?"

Jan nodded bleakly. "Dr. Vogle suggested that himself." Her eyes met Sheila's again. "But you know what, Sheila? I just have this feeling...." She

touched her chest. "Right here. The other doctors will say the same thing. I mean, my mother *died* of breast cancer. I was always predisposed to have it. Some women even have *healthy* breasts removed as a preventive measure." She shook her head sadly. "In the end, nothing is going to change. If I want to live to see my kids grow up, I'm going to have to have the surgery."

Sheila's eyes filled with tears again. She hated that she was so weepy. She knew she needed to be strong for Jan, but she couldn't seem to help herself. "Don't talk about not living," she said fiercely. "You're too important to all of us. And you know what? This isn't that bad. Thousands of women go through this and survive. In fact, they're stronger for the experience, because life is more precious and meaningful to them. Really, what will be so different afterward? Your body will be changed, but you'll still be Jan. You'll still have a wonderful husband who adores you and four wonderful children who also adore you and the rest of your family and friends." Sheila forced herself to smile. "And I've read that they do wonderful things with reconstructive surgery."

"I know, I know. Dr. Vogle said the same thing."

For a long moment, both were silent. Once again, Sheila realized how insignificant her problems were in relation to Jan's.

Finally Jan reached for Sheila's hand. "Thank you for coming." Her smile was wobbly as she

turned to look at Sheila. "I don't know what I'd do without you."

Suddenly Sheila knew she wasn't going to New York. How could she? She loved Jan. And Jan would need her a lot in the coming months. A lot of people needed her. This was where she belonged. So, as much as she'd like to run away and hide from her problems, she couldn't.

Come what may, she was going to have to stay right here in Rainbow's End and face them.

Chapter Thirteen

Saturday dawned clear and bright—a gorgeous spring day that was perfect for the company picnic. Sheila looked through her clothing to find the most comfortable outfit to wear, as well as the one that would most disguise her thickened waistline. She settled on black biker shorts because they had some give to them and an oversized cotton T-shirt that said God Created Eve Second Because Practice Makes Perfect on the front.

Looking at herself in the mirror, she realized the day was fast arriving when she would need to buy some maternity clothes. Which meant, whether she told them or not, everyone would soon know about the baby.

Including Jack.

What would he do when he realized what had happened? Would he think she had gotten pregnant on purpose...to trap him? But to think that would be ridiculous, given the fact he'd always used protection.

Maybe he would think someone else had gotten her pregnant. Deep down, Sheila knew that was a ridiculous thought, as well. Jack knew what kind of person she was. He'd said it himself. She didn't sleep around. No. He would know full well who the father of her baby was.

So the question remained. What would he do?

She had no idea. And today she was determined she wasn't going to worry about it, either. Tomorrow was soon enough to think about everything again and to make some concrete plans. During this picnic, she just wanted to enjoy herself and pretend that everything was fine, even if it wasn't.

She dreaded seeing Jack again, but she told herself it wouldn't be too bad, since there would be a lot of people at the picnic. She ought to be able to give Jack a wide berth. Still...just knowing he was nearby would be a strain.

Sheila sighed. Would it ever be easy to be around him? Would she ever get to the point where his presence didn't cause her pain?

She hoped so. She prayed so.

Because she wasn't sure anyone could endure this aching loneliness forever.

Jack got to the park at nine. The picnic officially started at ten, with the barbecue scheduled for

eleven-thirty and the games to begin at one.

When he arrived, the unmarried Callahan brothers were already there, and he helped them get everything set up. The company had rented the big pavilion for the day, and by the time the first attendees began to trickle in, the coolers were filled with beer and soft drinks, the chairs and tables were cleaned off and ready for use, and all the equipment for the games had been unloaded. One thing they hadn't had to worry about was food, because this year the meal was being catered and served by a local restaurant.

While he worked, Jack kept an eye out for Sheila's arrival. He told himself it wasn't that he was eager to see her. He just wanted to know when she came so that he could stay away from her.

About ten-thirty, he finally spotted her walking toward the pavilion. He couldn't help smiling. She was carrying a glove and wearing an Astros baseball cap, and she'd put her hair into a ponytail that was pulled through the opening of the cap. She looked about nineteen.

While he watched, she waved to someone in the distance, then turned to wait for them to catch up. As they neared, he saw it was Patrick and Jan, followed by their girls. Sheila and Jan hugged, and then they all walked toward the pavilion together.

Because he didn't want to be caught looking at her, he turned and began talking to Kevin. But he was acutely aware of her presence, and when a rea-

sonable amount of time had passed, he turned and pretended to see her for the first time. Smiling, he walked over to the group.

"'Bout time you got here," he said to Patrick. "We've already done all the work."

"I'm no fool," Patrick said.

"Hello, Jan. Sheila. Girls." His eyes only met Sheila's for a second or two, but that was enough to remind him of things he'd rather forget. Things he couldn't understand why he hadn't *already* forgotten. Maybe she really *was* a witch, he thought in wry amusement.

A few minutes later, Sheila spied someone at the other end of the pavilion and after murmuring something to Jan, left the group. Jan and the girls wandered off soon after.

"Hey, Jack," called Kevin. "Wanna go pitch some horseshoes?"

"Sure."

"How about you, Patrick?"

"Yeah. Sounds good."

They each grabbed a can of beer, then headed toward the horseshoe toss. Jack congratulated himself. The worst had passed. He had seen Sheila, they'd spoken, and now he could relax and forget about her.

When it was time to eat, Sheila was glad Jan and the girls had chosen a table on the opposite end of the pavilion from the one where Jack was sitting. She'd had a hard enough time acting casual for those

few minutes when they'd first seen each other. She filled her plate with barbecue, potato salad, cole slaw and beans, grabbed a roll, added some sour pickles and jalapeño peppers, then headed for Jan's table.

"Anybody want anything to drink?" she asked after depositing her plate and utensils in the empty space next to Jana.

"We've all got ours," Jan said.

Sheila headed for the drinks. Just as she reached the table where they were sitting, Jack approached from the other direction. Steeling herself, she allowed her gaze to meet his.

He smiled down at her. "You look like a kid today."

"Do I?" Why did it still hurt so much to see him?

"Yep. No older than nineteen."

"It's an illusion." She reached for a drink.

"So how's the job going?"

"Great. Couldn't be better."

"Good. I'm glad to hear it."

"How about you? Are you enjoying working in Pollero?" *Are you enjoying being away from the sight of me?*

He shrugged. "It's a challenging project."

"That's good. Well, my food is getting cold. See you later." She smiled, then turned and walked away.

She was proud of herself. That was her first real hurdle, and she'd managed to get over it without losing her cool. Maybe this was a good sign. Maybe overcoming future hurdles would get easier. Maybe

the day would come when she could see Jack and feel nothing.

After rejoining Jan and the girls, Sheila forced herself to put Jack out of her mind and give her full attention to them. Jan looked better today, more at peace with herself and her situation, Sheila thought. And after they finished their lunch and the girls had taken off, Jan said as much.

"I'm sorry I was so weepy yesterday. I think it was the shock. I'm fine today."

"I'm glad," Sheila said.

Jan fiddled with her crumpled napkin. "I've decided. I'm going to have the recommended surgery."

Sheila reached over and squeezed Jan's forearm. After a moment, Jan covered Sheila's hand with her own. Once more Sheila reminded herself that her problems were insignificant in relation to Jan's.

After that, their conversation moved to lighter topics, which turned into a fit of giggles when Jan described a recent shopping trip with Briana and Allene.

Once their laughter subsided, Jan said, "You know, it's not easy raising kids, but it's definitely worth it." Her expression turned thoughtful. "I wouldn't give my girls up for the world."

Under cover of the table, Sheila touched her stomach. She wanted so badly to confide in Jan, to share her happiness and her fears, yet she knew she couldn't. Not yet. Not until she told her parents. They deserved to be the first to know.

''Hey, you two, you gonna sit here forever? We're gettin' ready to start choosing up sides for the softball game.''

Patrick walked over to his wife and put his arm around her. The smile he gave her filled Sheila with longing. Jan's health might not be the greatest right now, but the health of her marriage was terrific.

A few minutes later, they all headed over to the softball field, where the majority of the employees and their families had already gathered, with more arriving every minute.

''Ready to get your butt kicked?'' Kevin said, winking at Patrick.

''We'll see who does the butt kicking,'' Patrick answered among hoots and catcalls.

The brothers began choosing sides. Kevin's first three choices were Jack, Rory, and Keith. Patrick chose Glenn, Sheila, and Kenny Romero, who said he'd lettered in high school playing shortstop. The remainder of their teams were chosen quickly from among mostly male employees, although Kevin *did* choose Justine to play the outfield, which pleased Sheila.

The game started promptly at one. Kevin and Patrick had drawn straws, and Patrick's team was up first.

''Sheila, you're going to be the lead-off batter,'' Patrick said. ''Then Joe, then Kenny, and Glenn, you'll bat cleanup.''

Sheila grinned. She loved softball. When she was a kid, she had consistently made the all-star team.

One year her team had even gone to the state finals. She walked over to the bats and began lifting them to see how heavy they were. Choosing one, she ditched her cap for a hard hat, which they were using in lieu of helmets, then walked over to home plate.

As she'd expected, Jack was pitching for his team. She was glad for the distance between home plate and the pitcher's mound, otherwise she might have been nervous facing him. She stepped up to the plate, her team shouting encouragement as she spread her feet apart and bent over into her batter's stance.

"C'mon, Sheila, show 'em what you got," Patrick yelled from the sidelines.

Jack started out with a curve ball, which fooled her. She'd expected him to give her his fastball. She swung and missed.

"Stee-rike one," called Ed Bassett, who was serving as the umpire.

Sheila gritted her teeth. She dearly wanted to get a hit, especially because Jack was pitching. She gripped the bat tighter and narrowed her eyes.

This time she got Jack's fastball. She swung and missed.

"Stee-rike two!"

Damn. Planting her feet firmly, she tried to clear her mind of everything except the coming pitch, which she was sure would be another fastball.

"C'mon, Jack, you can do it," called one of his team mates.

Sheila concentrated, and this time, when the ball whizzed over the plate, her bat connected with it solidly. Unfortunately, she hit it straight at Jack, and he made an easy catch for their first out.

Sheila flung down her bat. She wasn't a good loser.

Two more outs followed easily, and Jack's teammates were gleefully taunting as they moved in from the field and prepared to go to bat.

Patrick was pitching for their team. Although he wasn't as talented a pitcher as Jack, he had a decent fastball and a nice slider. By the time the first inning was over, he'd struck out two batters, walked one and gotten the third out with a pop fly.

Sheila didn't have her second at-bat until the third inning. The score was 1-0 in favor of Kevin's team. She knew she'd be facing Jack's fastball on every pitch, for by now he was completely warmed up and into the rhythm of his game. She wanted a hit so badly she could taste it, and she knew the only way she was going to get it was not to be intimidated by the ball.

She swung and missed on the first pitch. The second pitch was ball one. The third pitch came in high, and she resisted the urge to swing. Ed called it ball two. The fourth pitch was low. She swung and just clipped the ball for strike two.

By now the bystanders were yelling encouragement to both Jack and Sheila, depending on their loyalties. Sheila took a deep breath, gearing herself for his fastball as Jack wound up. He caught her off

guard, for instead of another fastball, he gave her a curve ball. She swung and popped it behind her, just out of reach of the catcher, who stumbled trying to get it.

The yelling was louder now, and Sheila could see her nieces jumping up and down. She could even hear little Allene calling, "Aunt Sheila! Aunt Sheila! Get a hit! Get a hit!"

She assumed her stance, and for just a moment, her eyes met Jack's. Sheila gritted her teeth. She was determined to get a hit.

The fastball came like streaked lightning, close in. Sheila couldn't help it. She stepped out of the box.

"Baaaalll three!"

Sheila's supporters erupted into cheers. Jack took his cap off and shoved his free hand through his hair. He looked at Ed as if he couldn't believe he'd called the pitch a ball.

"C'mon, Jack, no mercy!" called out one of the bystanders.

"Yeah, smoke one by her," yelled someone else.

Jack looked at the crowd, then back at Sheila. He put his cap back on and grinned.

Stepping out of the box, Sheila grinned back. She was feeling pretty good about now. No one else had managed to get three balls out of Jack. And all at once, the contest was about more than getting a hit. It was about getting on with her life. It was about getting over Jack. She would do it if it killed her.

She stepped back into the box and raised her bat. "Okay, Jack," she muttered. "I'm ready."

* * *

Jack started his windup.

The crowd was cheering wildly. He couldn't stop smiling. That Sheila. She was really something. Look at her. She wasn't the least bit afraid of his fastball. She was practically daring him to give it his best shot. "Okay, darlin'," he murmured. "Here it comes." The ball shot out of his hand.

The next few seconds were a blur. The ball streaked to the plate, but instead of the swing Jack expected, the bat flew from Sheila's hands, and she fell to her knees.

For a split second, fear immobilized Jack. Then realization dawned. Sheila had been hit. She was hurt. Jack raced to her side, reaching her just as Patrick and the rest of Sheila's teammates did from the other direction. Everyone was shouting.

"Sheila!" Jack said, heart pounding. "Are you all right?"

"I—I..." Her eyes were clouded with pain. "You hit me." She was gripping her right hand.

"I know. God, Sheila, I'm sorry." He ran his hands through his hair, then gingerly touched her shoulder. "Is it your hand?"

Sheila winced and nodded. "M-my wrist."

By now most of the spectators had crowded around them, including Sheila's parents, who were visibly upset. Sheila tried to reassure them that she was okay, but Jack could see that she was hurting big-time.

"Can you move it?" somebody asked.

"No, don't try," someone else said. "There might be broken bones."

"We need to take her to the hospital and get that hand x-rayed."

Jack was cursing himself. How could he have thrown the ball that hard? And especially at Sheila? What if it had hit her face? He swallowed. He would never forgive himself if she had any permanent damage. "It was my fault," he finally managed to say. "I'll take her."

"You don't have to take her," Sheila's father said. "I'll take her."

"No, I insist," Jack said.

"You stay and finish the game. Her mother and I will take her. Can you stand, Sheila?"

"I can stand," Sheila said.

The last thing Jack wanted was to stay and finish the game. He had no heart for it now, not after seeing the pain in Sheila's eyes. Not after knowing he'd put that pain there. He wanted to tell her father this. He wanted to push everyone else away and lift Sheila up into his arms and carry her to his truck. And after the hospital, he wanted to take her home and put her to bed and take care of her.

But he could do none of this, because he had no rights where Sheila was concerned. So he had to stand there helplessly and watch while her parents, one on either side, helped her off the field.

Sheila had taken her pain medication and was resting on her bed. She was thinking about her ig-

nominious exit from the picnic. The only good part of what had happened today was Jack's obvious concern about her welfare. Not that she was kidding herself that it meant anything. He would probably have been concerned no matter who he'd hit.

Sheila touched her stomach. It had been awkward having her parents with her at the hospital, but thankfully, they hadn't gone into the X-ray room with her. Her mother had wanted to, but Sheila had said she was fine and didn't need Rose to come along. If her mother had insisted, Sheila wasn't sure what she would have done, because she knew she had to tell the X-ray technician that she was pregnant. It would be too dangerous to have an X ray without protecting the baby. It all worked out, though, and her parents were none the wiser.

The X rays showed that she'd broken her wrist, so they'd wrapped it and put a cast on to immobilize it. She guessed it was a good thing she'd already decided she was going to have to give up working on the crew, because this injury would have prevented her doing so for at least six weeks, according to the doctor who had treated her.

Sheila closed her eyes. Another thing the doctor had told her was that the pain medication would make her sleepy. Good, she thought as she began to doze off. She would rather not have to think, anyway.

Just as the thought formed, her doorbell pealed. Heart pounding, she jolted awake. What in the world? Who could *that* be? She'd bet it was Carrie.

Sighing, she swung her legs off the bed and headed for the living room.

Reaching the front door, she was all prepared to tell Carrie that much as she loved her, she wasn't in the mood for company right now. Without even looking out the peephole, Sheila yanked open the front door.

Her mouth dropped open. Jack. It was Jack.

"Sheila." His gaze dropped to her right hand. He wet his lips. Looked up again.

Their eyes locked.

He swallowed. "Sheila," he said again. His voice sounded odd. Hoarse and unlike him.

And then, suddenly, she was in his arms.

"Sheila, I..." He broke off. Laid his head against hers. "I couldn't stop thinking about you," he murmured against her hair.

Sheila's heart was careening madly. She couldn't think straight. Jack. Jack was here. Jack was holding her. Tears blurred her eyes, and she trembled.

"You're cold," he said.

"No, no. I..." She couldn't go on. What did this mean? Why was he here?

Releasing his hold, he shut the door behind him, then gently led her to the couch. "Sheila, maybe it's too late. Maybe you'll tell me to take a hike, but I have to try."

All she could do was stare at him.

"Sheila, I...when you left today, I—I could hardly stand it. I wanted to go with you. For the rest

of the day I couldn't think about anything else but you and if you were all right."

Sheila could hardly breathe.

Jack stroked her cheek. "That was when I realized something. I love you, Sheila. For a long time, I've been denying the way I felt, but today I couldn't deny it any longer. I love you, and if you'll have me, I want to spend the rest of my life with you."

Sheila's lower lip trembled, and tears filled her eyes. Inside, she was quaking with a combination of happiness and stunned disbelief. Had she really heard him correctly? Had he really said he loved her?

Searching her face, Jack said, "Is there a chance for me?"

"Oh, Jack," she cried, finally finding her voice. "Yes. Yes, there's a chance for you." She smiled through her tears. "I—I love you, too. I've always loved you."

His smile took over his entire face. He tipped her head up and kissed her, a sweet, lingering kiss. Then he said, "I've got to do this right."

Letting go of her, he got down on his knees in front of her. Taking her good hand in his, he looked up into her eyes. His were filled with love as he said, "Miss Callahan, will you do me the honor of becoming my wife?"

Heart filled to bursting, Sheila cried, "Yes, yes, yes."

And then she was back in his arms. When his lips

lowered to hers, she sighed and gave herself up to his kiss.

"Jack?"

"Um?"

It was much later, but Sheila was still cradled in Jack's arms. She'd fallen asleep and he hadn't had the heart to wake her, so even though it was uncomfortable for him, he hadn't tried to move her off the couch.

She raised herself up to a sitting position.

Looking at her, he smiled. Her hair was all tousled, she had no makeup on, and her eyes were puffy from sleep. But she was still the most beautiful woman he'd ever seen, and she always would be. God, how he loved her. He couldn't believe he'd ever thought he didn't. It scared him to think how close he'd come to losing her entirely. In fact, he was damned lucky she hadn't thrown him out tonight. She'd have been within her rights to call him a pigheaded idiot and say she never wanted to see him again. But she hadn't, and he would be forever grateful that instead of the solitary life he'd imagined he wanted, he would instead get to spend it with this warm and wonderful woman who had made him a better man for knowing her.

"Jack," she said again, "pay attention. I have something to tell you."

He smiled again and kissed the tip of her nose. "I'm paying attention."

Taking his hand, she placed it on her stomach. "Um, how do you feel about having kids?"

"Kids?" For a few seconds, panic threatened. Then he relaxed. "Well, it'll take an attitude adjustment, but I guess...sometime in the future...kids would be okay." A little girl like Sheila. That wouldn't be so bad, would it?

"How far in the future?" she said.

There was a funny gleam in her eyes. He frowned. "I don't know. A couple of years?"

"Um, how about...five months?"

He stared into her eyes. For a long moment, there was no sound in the room save for the beating of his heart and the echo of her words reverberating in his head. "F-five months?" he finally stammered. "Are you...?'

She nodded. "Yes," she whispered. "I am."

This time the panic lasted less than a second. As the full realization of her revelation sank in, Jack's heart expanded until it felt as if it filled his entire chest. A child. *His child.* Almost reverently, his hand moved against her stomach.

Later, after the shock had worn off, Jack thought how funny life was. Yesterday he had wanted nothing more than to be free of even the thought of Sheila, not to mention any kind of lasting commitment. Today he couldn't wait to begin their life together and was eagerly looking forward to the birth of their first child.

He was the luckiest man in the entire world.

* * *

May 10

From the pages of the *Rainbow's End Register:*

Sheila Rose Callahan and John (Jack) Brady Kinsella were united in marriage Thursday evening in the chapel at Holy Family Church. Wearing her mother's lace wedding dress and a delicate lace veil from Ireland that had once been worn by her great-grandmother, Sheila carried a white prayer book covered with pink baby roses. The groom wore a gray tuxedo with matching gray cummerbund. He said he chose the color to match his bride's beautiful eyes.

Attendants were maid of honor Carrie Ferguson, who wore a pink silk-crepe dress and matching pink hat, and best man Michael Kinsella, the groom's brother, who wore a tuxedo identical to the groom's.

After the ceremony a small reception was held at the home of the bride's parents. After a honeymoon in New York City, the newlyweds will make their home in Rainbow's End.

August 27

From the pages of the *Rainbow's End Register:*

Sheila Kinsella (the former Sheila Callahan), gave birth to a boy yesterday afternoon at Tri-

City General Hospital. Ryan Patrick Kinsella arrived at 12:10 p.m. and weighed in at 7 lbs. 6 ozs. The proud father, Jack Kinsella, was passing out cigars at Pot O' Gold into the wee hours of the morning.

The new baby's grandparents are lifelong Rainbow's End residents Patrick and Rose Callahan (Patrick is the owner of Callahan Construction Company), and former residents Brady Kinsella, who now lives in Belle Vista, Arkansas, and Dorothy Kinsella, now residing in Houston.

Congratulations to all.

* * * * *

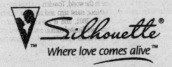

SILHOUETTE'S 20TH ANNIVERSARY CONTEST
OFFICIAL RULES
NO PURCHASE NECESSARY TO ENTER

1. To enter, follow directions published in the offer to which you are responding. Contest begins 1/1/00 and ends on 8/24/00 (the "Promotion Period"). Method of entry may vary. Mailed entries must be postmarked by 8/24/00, and received by 8/31/00.

2. During the Promotion Period, the Contest may be presented via the Internet. Entry via the Internet may be restricted to residents of certain geographic areas that are disclosed on the Web site. To enter via the Internet, if you are a resident of a geographic area in which Internet entry is permissible, follow the directions displayed on-line, including typing your essay of 100 words or fewer telling us "Where In The World Your Love Will Come Alive." On-line entries must be received by 11:59 p.m. Eastern Standard time on 8/24/00. Limit one e-mail entry per person, household and e-mail address per day, per presentation. If you are a resident of a geographic area in which entry via the Internet is permissible, you may, in lieu of submitting an entry on-line, enter by mail, by hand-printing your name, address, telephone number and contest number/name on an 8"x 11" plain piece of paper and telling us in 100 words or fewer "Where In The World Your Love Will Come Alive," and mailing via first-class mail to: Silhouette 20th Anniversary Contest, (in the U.S.) P.O. Box 9069, Buffalo, NY 14269-9069; (In Canada) P.O. Box 637, Fort Erie, Ontario, Canada L2A 5X3. Limit one 8"x 11" mailed entry per person, household and e-mail address per day. On-line and/or 8"x 11" mailed entries received from persons residing in geographic areas in which Internet entry is not permissible will be disqualified. No liability is assumed for lost, late, incomplete, inaccurate, nondelivered or misdirected mail, or misdirected e-mail, for technical, hardware or software failures of any kind, lost or unavailable network connection, or failed, incomplete, garbled or delayed computer transmission or any human error which may occur in the receipt or processing of the entries in the contest.

3. Essays will be judged by a panel of members of the Silhouette editorial and marketing staff based on the following criteria:

    Sincerity (believability, credibility)—50%
    Originality (freshness, creativity)—30%
    Aptness (appropriateness to contest ideas)—20%

   Purchase or acceptance of a product offer does not improve your chances of winning. In the event of a tie, duplicate prizes will be awarded.

4. All entries become the property of Harlequin Enterprises Ltd., and will not be returned. Winner will be determined no later than 10/31/00 and will be notified by mail. Grand Prize winner will be required to sign and return Affidavit of Eligibility within 15 days of receipt of notification. Noncompliance within the time period may result in disqualification and an alternative winner may be selected. All municipal, provincial, federal, state and local laws and regulations apply. Contest open only to residents of the U.S. and Canada who are 18 years of age or older, and is void wherever prohibited by law. Internet entry is restricted solely to residents of those geographical areas in which Internet entry is permissible. Employees of Torstar Corp., their affiliates, agents and members of their immediate families are not eligible. Taxes on the prizes are the sole responsibility of winners. Entry and acceptance of any prize offered constitutes permission to use winner's name, photograph or other likeness for the purposes of advertising, trade and promotion on behalf of Torstar Corp. without further compensation to the winner, unless prohibited by law. Torstar Corp and D.L. Blair, Inc., their parents, affiliates and subsidiaries, are not responsible for errors in printing or electronic presentation of contest or entries. In the event of printing or other errors which may result in unintended prize values or duplication of prizes, all affected contest materials or entries shall be null and void. If for any reason the Internet portion of the contest is not capable of running as planned, including infection by computer virus, bugs, tampering, unauthorized intervention, fraud, technical failures, or any other causes beyond the control of Torstar Corp. which corrupt or affect the administration, secrecy, fairness, integrity or proper conduct of the contest, Torstar Corp. reserves the right, at its sole discretion, to disqualify any individual who tampers with the entry process and to cancel, terminate, modify or suspend the contest or the Internet portion thereof. In the event of a dispute regarding an on-line entry, the entry will be deemed submitted by the authorized holder of the e-mail account submitted at the time of entry. Authorized account holder is defined as the natural person who is assigned to an e-mail address by an Internet access provider, on-line service provider or other organization that is responsible for arranging e-mail address for the domain associated with the submitted e-mail address.

5. Prizes: Grand Prize—a $10,000 vacation to anywhere in the world. Travelers (at least one must be 18 years of age or older) or parent or guardian if one traveler is a minor, must sign and return a Release of Liability prior to departure. Travel must be completed by December 31, 2001, and is subject to space and accommodations availability. Two hundred (200) Second Prizes—a two-book limited edition autographed collector set from one of the Silhouette Anniversary authors: Nora Roberts, Diana Palmer, Linda Howard or Annette Broadrick (value $10.00 each set). All prizes are valued in U.S. dollars.

6. For a list of winners (available after 10/31/00), send a self-addressed, stamped envelope to: Harlequin Silhouette 20th Anniversary Winners, P.O. Box 4200, Blair, NE 68009-4200.

Contest sponsored by Torstar Corp., P.O. Box 9042, Buffalo, NY 14269-9042.

PS20RULES

ENTER FOR A CHANCE TO WIN*

Silhouette's 20th Anniversary Contest

Tell Us Where in the World
You Would Like *Your* Love To Come Alive...
And We'll Send the Lucky Winner There!

Silhouette wants to take you wherever your happy ending can come true.

Here's how to enter: Tell us, in 100 words or less, where you want to go to make your love come alive!

In addition to the grand prize, there will be 200 runner-up prizes, collector's-edition book sets autographed by one of the Silhouette anniversary authors: **Nora Roberts, Diana Palmer, Linda Howard** or **Annette Broadrick**.

DON'T MISS YOUR CHANCE TO WIN!
ENTER NOW! No Purchase Necessary

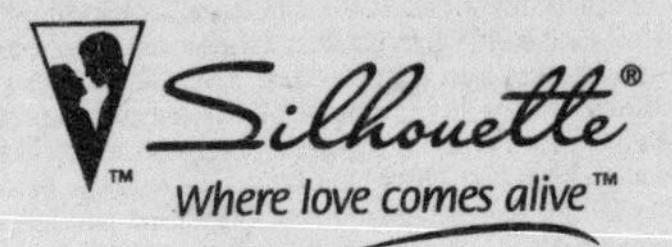

Name:

Address:

City: State/Province:

Zip/Postal Code:

Mail to Harlequin Books: **In the U.S.**: P.O. Box 9069, Buffalo, NY 14269-9069; **In Canada**: P.O. Box 637, Fort Erie, Ontario, L4A 5X3

*No purchase necessary—for contest details send a self-addressed stamped envelope to: Silhouette's 20th Anniversary Contest, P.O. Box 9069, Buffalo, NY, 14269-9069 (include contest name on self-addressed envelope). Residents of Washington and Vermont may omit postage. Open to Cdn. (excluding Quebec) and U.S. residents who are 18 or over. Void where prohibited. Contest ends August 31, 2000.

PS20CON_R

Dear Reader,

Happy 20th Anniversary, Silhouette! And Happy Valentine's Day to all! There are so many ways to celebrate…starting with six spectacular novels this month from Special Edition.

Reader favorite Joan Elliott Pickart concludes Silhouette's exciting cross-line continuity ROYALLY WED with *Man…Mercenary…Monarch,* in which a beautiful woman challenges a long-lost prince to give up his loner ways.

In *Dr. Mom and the Millionaire,* Christine Flynn's latest contribution to the popular series PRESCRIPTION: MARRIAGE, a marriage-shy tycoon suddenly experiences a sizzling attraction—to his gorgeous doctor! And don't miss the next SO MANY BABIES—in *Who's That Baby?* by Diana Whitney, an infant girl is left on a Native American attorney's doorstep, and he turns to a lovely pediatrician for help….

Next is Lois Faye Dyer's riveting *Cattleman's Courtship,* in which a brooding, hard-hearted rancher is undeniably drawn to a chaste, sophisticated lady. And in Sharon De Vita's provocative family saga, THE BLACKWELL BROTHERS, tempers—and passions—flare when a handsome Apache man offers *The Marriage Basket* to a captivating city gal.

Finally, you'll be swept up in the drama of Trisha Alexander's *Falling for an Older Man,* another tale in the CALLAHANS & KIN series, when an unexpected night of passion leaves Sheila Callahan with a nine-month secret.

So, curl up with a Special Edition novel and celebrate this Valentine's Day with thoughts of love and happy dreams of forever!

Happy reading,

Karen Taylor Richman,
Senior Editor

"I don't think we should see each other anymore,"

Jack said. To his credit, he looked her straight in the eye.

Sheila's heart began to pound. "I see."

"You're a wonderful girl, Sheila, but—"

"Is this because you're my older brother's best friend? Or are you just tired of me?"

"Sheila," he said softly. "I'm just trying to make it easier for you. It's just that I know I'm not the settling-down kind. And you are."

Sheila tried to contain her feelings. "I went into this relationship wide open. And I'm old enough to make my own decisions." Somehow she managed a little smile. "And you know something else, Jack. I think you're the one who's going to be surprised. Because you're going to miss me.

"In fact, you have no idea how *much*..."